From the Streets to the Sanctuary

By:
Eric "Corleone" Bledsoe

Cadmus Publishing
www.cadmuspublishing.com

Dedication

To that special mother that gave me life, Lois Harmon, I love you. And I would like to thank my family for having faith in me as I went through my trials and tribulations; because their unwavering love and support got me through them hard times... A special thanks to my Aunt Sarah, "Rest In Power", my aunts Jean, Doris, Gwen, Virginia, and Georgia.

Also, I want to thank my cousins for their love for me when I didn't have any self-esteem to excel; Thanks Regina "Rest In Power", Tonya, Kimberly, Victoria, Kharmen, and Ashley. A special thanks to my cousin Kelvin, "Get Well Soon" and "Stay Strong". I thank my wonderful sister, Tiwnda, for always being there for me in tough times; I thank my wonderful brotha, James, for being by my side as well.

Most of all, I send a special thanks to my princesses and princes, Marquita, Mikayla, Arthur, and Ladarrius for their love and joy they gave their daddy, Eric; And my baby's mother, Veronica.

I send a shout out to these individuals who have always been astounding friends to me over the years; Danielle May, Erica Sykes, Lakesha Johnson, Angel Coleman, Mishawndra Evans, Tiffany Taylor, Keishia Harris, Keisha Rudgley, Kesha Hayes, Keisha Evans, Tameka Glover, Kimberly Gales, LaTasha McClatchey, Jada Banks, Jontae Lattimore, Stacy Christian, and Karen Pate, who I am happy to see successful.

Also, the new friends I've met over the years of my incarceration; Ms. Whitaker, a loving and humorous empress; Ms. Dailey, a wonderful mother; and Ms. B, that special queen my heart yearns for because of her immaculate spirit.

I love you all dearly.

Introduction

Tee was an ordinary man living the street life since the age of 10. He started to adopt the ways of a thug by the peers in his community. That's when he began to shoot dice, sell dope, and pimp women to survive the streets.

Tee met back up with a childhood friend in jail. His name was Tony, and he had introduced him to a life of crime on the streets.

Tony took Tee to meet Jay who was the brick man in the haven and Tee began to get too deep in the game that he lost his sight on love and happiness with his woman.

Due to the constant struggles living that thug life the government seen that Tee changed his life to be a true black man of honor, loyalty, love, and respect.

When he took on the movement called "Purple Team Family," the government used an informant to get Tee back in the system.

Based on a true story of a man who was used as bait until he found his path and achieved that life of joy, peace, and love.

Prologue

It's 3:00 PM and Tee has just woken up from a long night in the streets with Jay, Stephanie, Caramel Mocha (Tee's wife)… and things seem a little far-fetched for the day.

"Good morning my queen!"

Carmella replied, "Good morning to you King."

Tee said in return, "What are you cooking for breakfast?"

She stated, "We having waffles and eggs love!"

"Alrighty then!" So, Tee went to the bathroom to get his hygiene in tat. While in the bathroom, he saw something from the bathroom window that stunned him. He saw two men trying to break in his neighbor's house. So, he waited until he was finished with his hygiene completely.

Once he came out the bathroom, he went downstairs where his wife was in the kitchen. He told Carmella that some thieves are breaking in the neighbor's house.

Carmella said, "What shall we do about it?"

Tee said in a confusing voice, "I really don't want to be labelled as a snitch; but we can't allow that to happen my love."

"Let's go take them down," Tee stated vigorously to his wife.

She replied, "Let's go then my king," and they left out the house and went to help their neighbors immediately.

The men saw them. They ran off as fast as they could, and then Tee and his wife waited til their neighbors came home; then told them what had happened.

So, their neighbors said to them, "We are so thankful for you all's help."

They replied, "It's no problem; that's what neighbors are for, right?"

The neighbors replied, "Yeah!" Afterwards they said, "Do you all want to come to dinner tonight?"

Tee replied, "What are you all cooking for dinner tonight?"

The neighbors stated, "Whatever you all have taste for, Tee!"

Tee replied, "I want to have steak and potatoes if you all don't mind."

"Okay neighbor! We really appreciate your help and lookout for us…"

Now that Tee has gotten recognition for his help in the community he stays in, he's happy to know that people are not stubborn where he lives in Memphis, Tennessee. I hope that his stature of being a peacemaker will continue in the coming years of his freedom from prison.

CONTENTS

CHAPTER 1

"Come on eight, locking for two blockhead brothers," Tee said while shaking the dice and wishing this roll would be the lick.

It was a lot of money in the pot, and he needed it because Tee had lost about $50 and he was down to about $250.

It was about $480 in the pot and only if Tee could hit that eight. The dice exited his hands and it felt like it was going to land on 5-trey, so he called it out, "Come on!"

"Damnit, 5-trey." One of the dice stopped on four while the other one landed on the other four and that was just what he needed.

He instantly jumped up and grabbed his money from under the rock then counted out $480 as he shoved it in his pocket.

"Damn, nigga."

"You ain't gonna give a brotha a chance to win his money back?"

"Bro, I got to go to pick up baby from work, I don't mean no harm."

"I'll stay here all day if one of you niggas gonna give me a place to stay."

"Man, you on some more stuff." So Tee said, "I got to go," heading out the door.

Tee's car wasn't really nothing to brag about, but it was purple and gold with a system that bangs from up the street to the bottom of the street.

He got in and closed the door. Even though Tee's car was the colors of the Lakers people always said, "It's clean!"

Before he cranked it up, he sat there for two minutes to make a sale. Then he cranked up his pimp mobile, and as soon as he cranked it up Tony walked up and pecked on the passenger side window.

"What's up, bro?" Tee asked. Tony stated that he needed a ride to his mother's house. "Bro, come on!" Tee replied. Tony jumped in the passenger seat and then looked at Tee and smiled. Then Tee said, "Why in the world are you smiling at me, brotha? I ain't your woman!"

Tony replied, "I'm thinking about Stephanie last night." Then Tee drove off and started listening to Tupac Shakur's "Ghetto Gossip." That's when they began to bob their heads to the music.

When Tee pulled up at Lanetta's job on time he decided to drop Tony off after he picked up Lanetta King.

Tony stayed in the Winbranch right down from Tee in Black-haven zone, and that's the hood. But it's good to get out of the hood 'cause in Tee's hood stuff gets really, really crazy.

It was 4:30 p.m. and that was the time that she clocked out, so he had pulled up at 4:25 p.m., but she couldn't leave until they let her. They sat in the parking lot for five minutes then Shay, Lanetta, and some more people came walking out the building.

Lanetta told Tony to get his butt in the back seat, so he opened the door and spoke to Lanetta as he jumped in the back.

Lanetta asked, "What you've been doing all day?" as soon as she got into the car.

The words hit Tee in the ear then his heart, so Tony started laughing!

Tee looked to see what her look was like because if she's looking mad because this nigga is laughing, I'm going to kick his butt.

She stared at Tee like he was a show on Lifetime.

"What did you say?" Tee said. "What did I do now?"

She replied, "I asked a question, baby."

"I shot dice at the Trap house and I won," Tee replied instantly.

She then said, "What you mean, that's all?"

Tee said, "That's enough!"

"What I tell you about that stuff?" Lanetta stated.

"You always take the li'l money we got and mess it off some kind of way, Tee."

"But baby…" he tried to speak.

"Baby my butt, nigga!"

"I need cigarettes for the week," Tee said. "I got some cigarettes." Then he pulled out his Newports and handed her the pack.

She took one out and fired it up then put the pack in the ashtray. From the back seat Tony asked, "Can I get yo short, Lanetta?"

Tee wanted to tell him "Hell no" but he knew she was going to do that herself.

"Nigga, you need to get a damn job. You always want something, and the next thing you gone want is a dollar. Man, times ain't just hard on you, they hard on all of us," Lanetta said angrily.

"Baby, give your friend a damn cigarette," she said, looking upside his head.

Tee pulled up at the gas station to get some gas and told Tony, "Nigga, you can work for this free ride and cigarette."

Tee pulled all the money out of his pocket and Lanetta's eyes lit up. That's when she said, "Where you get all that money from, baby?"

Tee replied, "You want it?" He flexed a hand full of cash that was nothing but big faces.

Tee answered, "Shooting dice," handing Tony a $100 bill. "Pump that for me, my brotha," Tee stated as Tony got out of the car.

"Baby, so you won that in the dice game this time?" she replied.

Tee said, "I tried to tell you, but you were so mad that I just let you continue to feel yourself."

She said to him, "Shine." Then she said, "Baby, I just get sick of you leaving the house with all we got and don't come back with nothing."

"I feel you, baby. We ain't going through that today so let that stuff stay where it's at, baby. No drama, okay, sweetie?"

"Okay, baby," she replied.

By the time Tony was walking back to the car Tee took a cigarette out the pack and gave it to Tony. As he got back into the car, he fired it up.

"What you planning on doing today?" Lanetta asked.

Tee said, "I don't have anything planned, babe. Do I need to?"

"No!"

"Why did you ask me that?" Tee replied.

"We need every dime you got to last us because that's our problem, baby," she said. "We mess off too much money in these streets and when I'm not working, babe. We need to just put it up and pretend it's just a normal day that we don't have any money."

Knock, knock, knock.

"It's five o'clock a.m. and who in the hell is knocking on my damn door at this time of morning?" Tee said angrily. He got up in his short pants and headed to the front door. He took a look out the peephole and noticed a face he'd never seen before.

"Who in the hell is this?" he said to himself.

"Who is it?" he said through the door as a voice said "My name is Corey. Is Lanetta home?"

"What the hell this nigga could want with my girl?" Tee thought angrily.

"She sleep!" Tee replied through the door and asked can he take a message?

"When would be the best time to come back?"

Tee told him to hold on and Corey said, "Okay," and that's when Tee opened the door.

Why is this corny-ass man standing before me? This couldn't be the man that I thought she would cheat on me with, but what the hell could this nigga want?

Tee was standing face to face with him like a gangsta should. A man he didn't know or wanted to know.

Tee said, "What's the deal? Lanetta is my girl. What the hell you need with her that you can't tell me, boy?"

"Nothing much," Corey said, "It's just that it wouldn't be right for me to deliver important information through someone other than a family member."

"Okay. I'll respect that, my nigga," Tee said. "You can come back around 2:30 or 5 p.m."

"Thanks, mister," Corey stated. "What's yo name?"

Tee said, "That's enough information for you because I have none for you."

Lanetta's voice was in his ear when she asked, "Baby, who was that at the door?"

When Tee made it back to the bedroom he was mad as hell, then he replied, "I don't know, but he asked for you and his name is Corey. He could not leave no information with me, baby."

Then she asked, "What did you say to him, babe?"

Tee replied, "I said I'll respect that and he could come back later around 2:30 or 5 p.m."

"Okay. Now come here, Tee."

"Hell no! You need to tell me who this dude is because ain't no suckas going to be coming up to my door and asking for my woman and shit, ya dig? I ain't no sucka, Lanetta, I'm a fuckin' gansta, stupid-ass cunt. You better be glad that I was cool because I started to smack his ass in the head with my P98 Ruger. Baby, you need to let me know what the hell going on between you and this nigga because I'm not the one to play with at all."

Lanetta said, "Tee, I'm sorry, baby! It's just the man I supposed to buy my stamps from," Lanetta stated. "Baby, I know that you don't get yo stamps 'til next week, and that's why I was tryin' to buy his right now." She then said, "I know that you forgot that we have a light bill to pay before the week is out."

"So, are you gone get the money for the stamps early?" Tee asked.

She then replied, "I told him to come today, and we don't need them if you got enough to pay it, baby."

"Hell, I got enough to pay it for about three to six months or so, so don't let that stuff happen again, baby, or it's gone be some repercussions."

"Yes, baby," she replied. "You so damn crazy, and I love you, Tee."

She got up and went in the kitchen to fix some breakfast with her bra and booty shorts on, standing 5 feet 8 inches tall and weighing 110 pounds.

Yeah, she has a Kelly Rowland type shape, Tee thought. "That's my queen!" Tee replied.

When she turned around knowing Tee was looking at that diamond cut in between her legs she started blushing at the fact that he was focused on her sexiness.

"What's for breakfast?" Tee asked. "Pancakes, eggs, and grits?"

"I don't know, babe, but it's whatever you want."

"I'll eat whatever."

She looked at Tee and smiled, then said, "Whatever, huh?" noticing that Tee was off his square. She walked into the kitchen while he watched her gorgeous body strut passionately to fix his food.

He grabbed the remote and laid there on the couch as he put the TV on the news, then he began looking at it, but not really paying any attention until they showed a very, very familiar house.

He sat up in the bed and turned up the volume. They said, "Last night around 7:45 p.m. a store got robbed on Winchester and Millbranch and Jackson and Watkins Road." The police said that two men were D.O.A. and the store owners were found dead. "The house behind the store is the house that belongs to the mother of Tony Talley," the police stated. "He was the last person on the camera, and they are looking for him for questioning."

"Damn!" Tee replied, thinking, "Tony is my nigga even though he's a pain in the ass, so I wonder did that nigga do that stuff the news said happened?"

Tee hoped Tony had sense enough to get out of Dodge because the feds would be looking for his ass. Tee jumped up from the bed and headed straight to the phone to call Tony's cell number. When he pressed the button to get a dial tone on the house phone he heard Lanetta and Shay laughing and talking.

"Hello," he said through the other end of the phone. "That's okay, I'll use the cell phone, Lanetta."

"Okay, baby," she replied.

Tee then put the house phone down and looked over to the small dresser looking for his cell phone. He didn't see it at all, so he exclaimed, "Goddamnit!" then got up and looked under the damn bed.

"What the hell wrong with ya, Tee?" Lanetta asked, walking behind him.

"You wouldn't believe it if I told you." While on his knees under the bed looking for the phone Tee began to enlighten her on the news about Tony. He then asked, "Where the hell is the other phone?"

Lanetta stated, "If it's that important to you then you can use this phone, baby." She told Shay that she will call her back later and handed Tee the house phone.

As he got up and sat on the end of the bed, Tee said, "The police is saying that Tony robbed and killed two people at the store by his house."

Lanetta asked Tee again, "What's wrong?"

He replied, "They after my homeboy." Tee dialed the number to Tony's phone and it rang two times then the answering machine picked up.

"Damn!" said Tee as he tried it again while Lanetta sat there waiting to comfort her man.

"Baby," hoping that Tony would answer the phone.

"What?" she replied.

Tee said, "The food!"

"Oh my!" Then she ran to the kitchen and that's when Tony answered the phone.

"Hello!"

Tee said, sounding like he just got up, "Bro, what the hell is going on?"

Tony replied, "Ain't nothing going on, Tee."

"But what you mean, bro? Look here, man."

"Listen to me! The police are looking for your butt in a major way."

"Damn, nigga, you talking like I killed somebody," Tony replied. He asked Tee, "How you know all this, bro?"

Stupid-ass boy! The stuff was all over the news and, "Where the hell were you at, anyway?" Tee replied.

"Ooh!"

"No, you didn't!"

"If the police department is looking for me like you say, why haven't they come to my mother's house?"

"By the way, you're charged with two counts of first-degree murder," as Tee cut him off to let him know that he was for real. Tee told him, "He are not the enemy, and don't go home to your mom's house unless you ready to turn yourself in."

After that, Tony hung up the phone. He never told Tee his location at all and Tee knew the reason. Tee was also being talked about in the streets as well on some robberies and murders.

Tony thought Tee might want to turn him in to the police, but the truth is Tee wouldn't do that stuff to one of his worst enemies. The truth is he don't want to be called a rat or even think that it's okay to turn someone in for a crime. Tee always kept it real with himself and the people he fooled with on a daily basis. He knew the price for a snitch and being one is not his steel-o at all.

So, Tee left it alone and told him to get ready to get in the back seat of the car so that his Cousin Shawn can get in the front seat. Tee finally headed to the east to drop that bag off with his cousin at Mike's house. When they got there Shawn told him to pick him up at around 8:30 p.m. and take him to the Haven on his way back home.

Tee replied, "Okay," and he drove off to meet his girl and her friend. Tee and Tony met up with Lanetta and Stephanie at the Mall of Memphis in East Memphis. Then they all went to the movies to see the "The Awakening" by Kevin Bacon. Once they got all their refreshments they went to sit down in their seats.

Tee told Lanetta that he was gone break her back tonight but Lanetta laughed. She said, "That won't be happening too fast 'cause she is on her period." Other than that, she would have told him to break her back.

While they were at the movies Tony and Stephanie went in the restroom to take care of their business because Stephanie had to go home to her man.

Tony wanted her so bad, so once he finally got the chance to fuck the shit out of Stephanie in the mall restroom inside the stall he was so happy to get that pussy. Tony put her legs so high on his shoulders and one leg on the floor as he stroked that juicy wet pussy in a circular motion. In and out until she began to moan in ecstasy. That's when Tony exploded inside her. When they got through doing it they both washed up in the sink, then they headed back to the movie where Tee and Lanetta were sitting to finish watching the movie.

Lanetta told Stephanie that she would have to get home before her man does, so Lanetta kissed Tee and said that she would meet him at the house after she dropped Stephanie off at home.

Tee said, "I love you, baby, and be safe, sweetheart, in those streets."

Lanetta replied, "Okay," and left the mall heading to Stephanie's house.

Tee and Tony jumped into Tee's whip and they headed to the Trap to pick Tee's cousin Shawn up and take him home. Tee asked, "Tony, was Stephanie's pussy good, and if so, why don't you just tell her to be your girl?"

Tony said, "I like it this way because I don't have to worry about the headaches."

Tee stated to him, "What headaches? The ones you get when women start acting like they own you because they just fucked you?"

"They expect more out of you," Tony said with virtue.

Tee was like, "Damn, man, you really are aware of how these women are these days, huh?"

Tony knew that was the only way to get into Stephanie's pants without even having any strings attached to him and her forever. He knew that his style was the essence to a woman that's already involved. When she gets tired of her man's dick she gone want Tony's dick.

Tony said, "That's smart on a man like me, cuz."

Tee sadly said to him, "Nigga, you better be careful dealing with her too because her nigga might catch you and her and then there goes your life. If that happens, I'm gone have to kill that nigga for you, cuz!"

Tony replied, "Tee, I'm smooth as ice and twice the fight, so he better watch out for this gangsta-and-a-half, ya dig?"

"Well, talk that shit later because we are here at Mike's crib now, cuz." Tee blew his horn and Shawn came running out of the Trap house. When he jumped into the car and seen that Tee and Tony were smoking that good kush he asked them could he hit it.

Tee then said to him, "Yeah, nigga." Tony passed him the blunt of that OG kush real quick.

Tee put the car in reverse and then drove to ball off into the sunset and hit the expressway headed to Blackhaven quickly.

"What's up, nigga?"

"I'm making it, Shawn, and I finally fucked Stephanie too in the movies last night," Tony said.

"Nigga, what you mean to tell me that you fucked Stephanie

in the movies?"

"Yeah!" Tony replied.

Shawn said, "That got to be a fucking miracle to get that opportunity."

They all tripped about it as Tee got mad at them because he can't get no pussy tonight.

Tee said, "I might can't get none, but she will be eating this muthafucker up all night."

The day is slightly ending and everyone is ready to get to their place to relax on their bed with their woman. They all felt exhausted and couldn't wait to see the doorsteps of their cribs.

Tee finally dropped everyone off and made it home to Lanetta. As he walked through the door and made it to the living room she had nothing on and told Tee, "Come on now, baby."

Tee smiled and hurried up and got in the bed and began to break her back as he said were gone do at the movies. Then as he entered inside her she moaned with a soft voice, "Oh, baby, right there, please."

Tee then stated, "Isn't this dick good to ya?"

"Yeah! Yeah!"

Tee get this pussy, baby. Tee and Lanetta finished making love and they both fell asleep.

When he and Lanetta woke up and realized that she was late for work, Tee got his keys and told her that he'll take her to work since it was his fault.

Tee went to crank up the car to let it warm up in the driveway as he and Lanetta went out the house to get in the car. Before he could pull off she put that Tupac Shakur "Ghetto Gossip" in the CD player and then put the car in reverse.

While backing up out of the driveway Tee seen Tony and he asked asked Tee if he could ride with them and Tee said, "Yeah." Then Tee drove off to drop Lanetta off at work. Tony asked

Lanetta could he start helping her at work for his community service?

She told him that it's cool as long as he's on time every day. Tony then asked Tee, "Can I have a cigarette?" and Tee told him to get a job in a laughing way, but Tony was a little upset. Tee gave him a cigarette and they drove off into the sunset to get money at the Trap house.

They made it to the Trap house and seen Jay and Mike sitting in there rocking up a brick of that pure cocaine. Tee said that he needed four and a split to get his grind on at the club.

Jay replied, "I'll give you that when I get through with this batch, homie," and Tee said it would make a great deal of money at his club. So, Jay asked Tony what he want to do about getting these dividends?

Tony replied, "Nigga, don't you know that I'm still on papers? But I do need to get a little extra money for the probation officer, though."

Mike was like, "Nigga, are you crazy doing that stupid-ass shit, nigga?"

Tony said, "I am not doing nothing no different than the rest of you all," and that's when Tee said, "Stop trying to drill my homeboy, Mike."

Jay was like if he want to do it he's a grown fuckin' man.

CHAPTER 2

It's been a month and Tony still had not been caught or had anyone turn him in, which is good because Tee wouldn't want no one to do that to him either. He told him that if he had not did anything then it's no reason to be running, and we're together every day.

Even though Tony be fuckin' some bitch that stay down the street from Tee's house he said he met on the chat line. Tony been with her for about a week and said that she was pretty cool but just big as hell. But hey, like Tony said, big girls need love too. Besides, where else could he go since the police had been over Tee's house looking for him already?

While Tee were in the Peppertree Apartments shooting dice, he ran into this freak named Sherita Smith and she asked Tee if he wanted to kick it with her in her apartment. Tee told her it would have to wait 'til he finish getting his money, and she said, "Here's my phone number, (901) 398-7816." She told him to call when he's on his way. Tee hit the dice game for $4,500 and then went to buy him some kush for $1,500. Afterwards he headed to Sherita's apartment in the apartment complex of the Peppertree.

When Tee walked in there and seen that she was dressed in her two-piece bra and panty set his eyes was like, "Damn!" Then he told her, "Roll up this blunt, beautiful."

As Sherita rolled up the blunt Tee watched her tongue while she licked the blunt in a seductive manner, then he got really hard. When Sherita seen how hard he had gotten from her licking that blunt she rolled it up, passed him the blunt, and went down on him.

She started sucking his dick with no hands and she twirled her tongue around his dick seductively and passionately. Tee was like, "Ooh, shit!" "Damn, your cap is fire as hell, girl!" So Tee became really fond of her oral sensation.

Tee knew that he is still wanted for his double murder and robbery with his crew and he felt the pleasure from Sherita's mouth massaging his dick. That is what gave him the thought of what he's going to miss if he get caught up. "I'm still wanted for a crime my crew did awhile back and that's why I'm stacking this paper so I'll be prepared to battle this crooked-ass system," Tee thought. Now that his mother isn't helping and trying to turn him in Tony can't even pay his phone bill. However, like Tony said, he don't need that joint anyway. Tee was so caught up in the dice game that he forgot to pick up his baby and take her to the workhouse.

Tee's phone started ringing so he answered it. "Hello," Tee said to the voice on the other end of the phone. "Nigga, you must be stupid or something because I need to get to work now," Lanetta said angrily.

That's when he said, "My car stop running and I'm getting it fixed at Jay's house." Then Tee told her to get Shay to come take her to work.

She then said, "Okay. Baby, I love you," and then she called Shay and told her to come pick her up for work, but before Lanetta and Tee hung up the phone she said, "Baby, I'm off to work," as she headed out the door.

The way she jumped in the passenger seat of Shay's 1994 Lexus ES 350 Coupe gave Shay the impression that she were mad at Tee.

Afterwards, Tee went ahead and got up and hopped into Jay's 1994 Lexus Coupe while he waited for his 2008 Dodge Charger to get fixed, then he headed back to the Winbranch Apartments where he spotted police cars everywhere.

Tee already knew what they was doing, but he still could not believe it. He sat on the hood of his car and fired up a cigarette. Not only did they take Tony to jail, they also had his girl Stephanie too.

"Damn!" he said to himself. Then he began to get back in the car and headed to the house. They could have let old girl make it, but Tee wondered what was the reason for them locking her up, anyway? "I guess the police the don't give a fuck. I'm glad that they didn't catch me in my spot because they could have took me and my girl to jail too."

Anyway, Tee's cigarette was getting close to the butt and he went to the house garage. Tee cut the car off as he stood up and got out of the car, then thumped his butt by the side of the garage near the boxes of the garage window. When it landed, he seen something that caught his attention and walked where the cigarette butt was and seen an empty Trojan packet.

Tee kicked it around trying to determine how old it was and who could have had it. Tee thought anybody else his age would think shit like that around the house that someone's cheating. He can't really say that Lanetta had that, and for one, he found this outside the garage door, and two, he have him a good girl. She be around him too much to cheat, so Tee thought he's not gone worry about it either. Tee kicked it one last time before he walked in the house, then looked down the street seeing that the police was cruising up the street looking for someone.

As he decided to enter his bedroom he discovered this Corey nigga hitting his girl from the back, and he was so fucked up that he pulled out his 40 Glock from the hallway closet, unlocked it, and loaded it as he aimed it straight at Corey's head as he released the whole clip in both of them.

Tee would have never thought that Lanetta would have disrespected him or their domain the way she did today. But one thing for sure, that won't happen again.

He walked out the house with all his belongings and headed towards North Memphis to hide out for awhile. He stopped at the gas station to get some gas and a box of cigars because he had a lot of pain in his heart.

So, after experiencing that shit he truly had no fuckin' remorse for what he did to Corey or Lanetta because she tried to play him like a sucker. Now the work is done, he decided to call Shay to see what's good in the hood. Even though they were best friends, he couldn't tell her he shot and killed Lanetta and Corey today.

Tee told her the police finally caught Tony, and on top of that, they took Stephanie to jail too.

Shay said, "You lying."

So, he said, "I wish I was, Shay."

Then she said, "That's fucked up, baby."

Tee then said, "I'm glad that they didn't catch me with him because I'm already hiding from those robberies and murders that took place a couple of years ago."

Shay then said, "I know, Tee, that's why Lanetta were making sure you stay out the streets because she didn't want to have to deal with the system. You feel me, Tee? Okay, then. I got to get back in the building before they fire me," as she hung up the phone.

Anyway, Tee stated he gone find him a job to cover up the dope money because he knew that he must get prepared before they snatch him up and take him to jail. However, he didn't know he fell into a deep, deep sleep because when he woke up he were looking in Shay's face.

She was so shocked to see him sleeping so hard that he asked her, "How the fuck did you get into my crib?"

Shay said that she found Lanetta and Corey dead in Lanetta's house in the bedroom, so she asked him, "Did you have anything to do with that shit, Tee?"

He said, "Hell, no," as he jumped up to put his clothes on like he was concerned, but Shay never knew that he had a thing for her since that nigga came to the house that day.

This was the perfect time to put his bid in since Shay was single and independent. Shay asked him, "What you are about to do?"

Shay followed him to his car, and when he got in the car she stated, "Tee, I always wanted a thug/gangsta type nigga. So many of them are inferior. Would you be that nigga, huh?"

After he heard that all types of shit scan his mind. Then he said, "Let me think on it."

Shay stated, "I know how close you and Lanetta were, Tee."

Tee said, "Please allow me enough time to recuperate from the tragedy I've experienced."

"Alright then," Shay replied, "but here's my number anyway, (901) 795-2909, and call me later, baby."

Tee replied, "When I call you later are we gone fuck or what?"

Shay said, "Do you really want me to answer that?" as she walked away from his car and jumped into hers.

Tee thought to himself, "That's cool," then he said to himself, "So we're going to fuck?" He cranked up his car, put it in drive, and drove off.

"It's so packed out here on these streets," he stated and cruised down the street. Niggas, crack heads, and whores were all over the streets in Smokey City on Hastings Circle."

He drove to the next street over to go over Jay's house and so he could get some weed too because he be pushing them bows on a daily basis. Tee had to go re-up and he had to stay on point, as well. Hopefully he can get them niggas to all pitch in to buy his dope because he was thinking all the way over there what can he do?

When he pulled up at Jay's spot he heard a voice call his name. "Tee! Hey, Tee!" somebody said, sounding like a girl. Tee looked and seen in his rearview mirror it was Tonya Sexy Red Ass and she always wanted Tee to be her man.

Tee was kind of afraid of her because of the rumors he heard in the streets. He knew that she have been tossed by several niggas in the neighborhood and that is why he always turned his head from that path with Tonya. What the hell did she want with him?

What's up, Tonya?" as he stepped out of the car.

Tonya said, "I seen Tory on the news. What the hell, man? Do you think that Tony did that stuff?"

"Man, I don't know, Tonya," Tee replied, "because I can't say."

"Where is your woman Lanetta?" she said excitedly. "I heard that someone shot and killed her and Corey two days ago."

Then Tee replied, "I know that when I find out who they ass is mine, Tonya." Tee angrily stated that with aggression as he walked inside Jay's house.

"What's up, Jay? What's crackin' with you, cuz?" Tee asked.

Jay said, "Shit, cuz, but pushing these pounds to the max. I'm gone try to see if I could get cuz to fuck with me for the 10 Gs."

Tee then asked Jay, "Where your homegirl at?"

Then Jay replied, "Who, Keisha?"

Tee said, "Hell, yeah."

"Man, at the house suckin' some nigga dick. You know that whore got her ass beat the last time you was over here, Tee."

"Oh, yeah."

The night Tonya and Keisha was stripping, "Yeah, nigga! Y'all had got them tipsy as hell. They be getting freaky when they get on that shit, cuz."

Tee replied, "Who you telling? I know they do." After he said that they went and sat on Jay's steps.

Tee rolled up a blunt of that loud Pak. Man, I was high as hell from that OG kush that I needed something to drink. Jay passed that 1800 bottle and he took a swig.

"What you got, Tonya?" as he looked at her, Jay replied, then he slid his scale close to him.

Jay picked up a plastic bag with what Tee figured was cocaine. He put some on the ID card and put it on the scale.

"Here ya go, Tonya," Jay said as she handed him the $10. Then Jay said, "I'm gone fuck with you too, and you know that you and old girl fuck with me."

When he said that, Tonya put a big-ass smile on her face because he put enough on the scale to make her happy for her $10. She got that shit and dipped out the door so damn fast, knowing she will be back as soon as that shit is gone.

"Oh, shit!"

"My nigga, you got to tell me about Tony crazy ass," Jay said, but for some reason Tee knew that was coming.

He turned the bottle of 1800 up as Jay asked him, "What

happened?"

Tee then stated, "I really don't know, cuz, but Tony told me that he didn't do it," Tee stated to Jay.

"Bullshit," Jay replied.

When he said that, Robert said he seen the nigga run out of the house that morning. Tee stated, "I don't know, bro, that's that nigga."

"Isn't that's ya boy?" Jay asked.

Tee replied, "If he was and he did a move, why did he tell me that he didn't do it if he's my boy? If he did, he shall have never hid it from me, like I'm going to snitch or something."

"Maybe that nigga telling the truth," Jay stated humorously.

"Mane."

"I got problems of my own to worry about, Jay," Tee replied.

Tee asked Jay for about four pounds of that kush. Then he said, "Can you help a nigga, Jay?"

"I'll see, my nigga," Jay replied. "You know I'll do what I can for my real homie." then he said, "Don't abandon your boy like that thought. Find out about him and make sure he's straight. You the only homie he mess with, Tee, real talk."

"You right," Tee replied.

Jay said, "Put his shoes on your feet." But little did Jay know, Tee was already in his shoes but haven't got caught yet. With that said, he sat back and did some thinking of his own and Jay was making a lot of sense. Thinking to himself, Tee thought he and Tony were homeboys and it wouldn't be right to leave him in the dark.

Tee got so messed up that day and left seeing two of everything on his way to the crib. Tee was like, that's really fucked up because Tony is his best friend from childhood years. To see him that fucked up made him realize that doing these crimes isn't the business, but Tee knew a nigga had to survive some kind of way in these streets. Mostly everybody will experience some things in their life that will have them in a rage or insane, but Tee want them to stay focused even when faced with those type of things.

Tee and Lanetta went through that stuff all the time when she was living, even though they always found a way out of no way to rise beyond those issues.

Tee always tell Tony to be patient and let things come to him, just as he tell all of his homies. Tee don't want nobody he fucked with to fall down around him or his family.

Shay called Tee in the kitchen to eat his breakfast, and she cooked him some waffles, eggs, and bacon with a cup of orange juice. Then she told him how much he meant to her and that she wanted them to spend the rest of their life together.

Tee replied, "I love you too, and I would love to be your king for life."

Then she stated, "For real, baby?"

Tee then said, "Hell, yeah!"

Shay replied, "When are we going to make this official, babe?"

Tee stated seriously, "On our anniversary. Our anniversary is on June 1, 1994, and that's when we will have our engagement party to be married as long as we stay on the same level as one, beautiful. I will be as loyal to you as you are to me."

So, Shay said, "Okay, sweetheart."

Tee actually was amazed because his ex-girlfriend's best friend wanted to marry him. He knew that woman wasn't who she seemed to be when he's not around. So, Tee prepared for the worst, and he wasn't stupid as she thought he were. By the way, Tee had his ducats ijust in order as the junkies have when they want a hit.

Tee was so smart about life's relationships from the past hurt and pain of losing his parents in a double homicide in 1993, a year before their 30th anniversary. This pain is why Tee have the ability to cipher any and every situation around him. Tee have a gift that were instilled from birth.

That is why Tony, Jay, Mike, Stephanie, Keisha, and that girl Princess loved him. If Tee would just change his life of crime, pimping, and dope selling he would by far be a force toward the government and the world. He have to find who he are and where's he's from as a black man. Once Tee discovers these attributes and begin to use them daily he will have that leadership that he wants with the street life

"Well!"

The phone rang. "Hello, who this is?"

"This Jay, cuz. I was wondering what you doing, homie?"

Tee replied, "I'm not doing nothing at the moment, but what's up?"

Jay said, "I wanted to know if you are ready to go on this mission we talked about last week?"

Tee replied, "Hell, yeah! Nigga, I'm always ready to get those dividends by any means necessary, and you shall know that, homie."

"Right on!" Jay said with enthusiasm. "Tee, I will meet you at the spot then in about a couple of hours."

"Okay!" Tee then hung up the phone.

Tee called his cousin house to see what Shawn was up to, but he didn't get an answer, so he went on to the Trap house where Jay be at in South Memphis.

Once he made it to the South Tee seen his other homie who was locked up with him in the county. Tee asked him, "How have you been since getting out of jail?"

Mario told him he have been great since getting the freedom he wanted to have back. Then he said, "Tee, it is truly an honor to see you on the town living, nigga! What have you been doing since you have been out, homie?"

Tee replied, "Cuz, I have been getting this money and fuckin' like a mad Russian in a war. This life has been lovely, homie. I supposed to be getting married soon to Shay, my high school sweetheart. Don't you remember her from Hillcrest High School?

Mario said, "I think so, homie."

"We are planning it next year if you want to come, homie."

"I know that you might want to kick it like we used to do in school because Jay, Stephanie, Keisha, Tony, and I still hang together as a family."

Tee stated, "Happily," to Mario.

"Well, I'll let you know more on that, Tee, when I talk to my woman later on tonight, cuz," Mario replied.

"Alright," Tee said with a smile on his face.

Tee told Mario that he will call him later to get some kush from him, and if he is still grinding like he use to in high school that he want 10 pounds of that OG, and that's for real.

The way Mario looked at Tee was a sign to him like, "nigga, we in public." Tee jumped into his car and then drove off to the crib.

When he got to the crib and seen Shay cooking in the kitchen, he said that he seen her cousin Mario at the job site.

Then Shay said, "What the hell was he doing there by himself anyway, baby?"

Tee replied, "I don't know, sweetie. All I do know is I'm hungry and I'm very, very tired from grinding in those streets."

"Well, baby, you need to take you a bath first and then come get you something to eat because I'll be through cooking by then, my king. I want you to be as comfortable as you need to be, my king," Shay replied happily.

CHAPTER 3

Sitting at the kitchen table, Tee begin thinking about everything that occurred that day Lanetta and Corey was in his bed.

Tee was finally sick of it, so he picked up the phone and called his old job. When they said that they had no openings, he walked out the house. It had been two days since he's been over Jay's house.

Tee couldn't get in touch with Shay, so he decided to go to visit his homie Tony Taller. Since downtown was 15 minutes from his house, he made that his next destination.

Tee passed a lot of pretty women on his way down to 201 Poplar Avenue, and some were riding while some were walking, but a hoe wasn't nothing to him.

So, he walked inside the visiting room and waited on Tony to enter. Tony finally came in and sat down, looking like a fool with his hair all over his face and head.

Tony grabbed the receiver to talk to me, "What's up, Tee?"

Tee said, "Same old, same old shit. So, how about you, cuz? How are you holding up in this hellhole?"

Tony replied, "Shit, my nigga, all I got to say is I'm holding on, but I'll be okay."

There was a moment of silence and then Tony asked Tee about the hood. Tee said, "The hood is good!"

While looking for the right time to ask him about the golden question, but before he could ask him, Tony said, "And no, I didn't do that shit."

Tee replied, "Cuz, I didn't ask you about that, homie, but it was coming."

"I don't know how I ended up in this shit," Tony stated. "I was at the hotel the day you call me, Tee. I haven't killed nobody, and I don't have no fuckin' money to prove my innocence. No lawyer or shit. I've been in this bitch 45 days and you are the second person who came to see me, Tee."

Then Tee asked, "Tony, what they do with old girl?"

Tony said, "Are you talking about my baby, Stephanie?"

"Yeah, Stephanie," Tee replied.

Then Tony said to him, "She still at Jail East."

"Oh! For real? That's fucked up," Tee said in shock. "What they get her for, anyway?"

Tony said, "She was harboring a fugitive."

"Damn, nigga!" Tee replied. "Anyway, I'm gone put a few dollars on your books to last you until I'm able to come back to visit you again. Tony, this is so you can have something for yourself and don't be having to ask them niggas in there for shit."

"Thanks, man!" Tony said. "I sure as hell needed that because I don't have nobody. and it's like nobody even cares about me at all." Then he stated, "If you knew how I feel you'll understand."

Then Tee stated, "I do a lot of thinking, and that's the reason I act the way I do. The fucked up thing about it is that I don't know if the way I am acting is really crazy. People tell me I'm crazy every day, all day, in and out of jail. Even though you tell me how crazy I am, but it's all good, Tony. You can do that and still feel okay because I feel like you are the only one that give a shit about me, and that's real, bro."

"Thanks for that, Tee," Tony replied. "That really made my day in this hellhole called jail. Also, my own mother don't even come up here to see me or write or shit, so thanks again, Tee. I really mean that too, Tee, from the bottom to the top of my heart, bro, and I hope that it's appreciative."

"Yeah!" Tee said, thinking about everything Tony said to him at visit. "Well, our time is up. I got to get to the house now, cuz, so until next time, keep your head up and out of the clouds. That's what's up!"

"Hey, Tee," stopping him in his tracks as he picked the receiver back up and placed it to his ear.

"Yeah?" Tee replied as Tony asked, "Can you go by my mom's house for me?"

"Yeah, nigga. You know I'll do that for you, cuz."

Tony told him to tell her he missed and loved her and that he haven't done nothing to nobody. "I don't have the address because I don't know it by heart but tell her I would love to hear from her."

"Okay, Tony," Tee said, "I'll do that, cuz," because he was feeling every bit of his pain.

Tee left out the jailhouse broke because he gave Tony every damn dime that he had in his pocket.

The outlook he had about Tony had changed. He never knew until now. He walked to his car and hopped in and shut the door as he stated to himself, "Tony will be alright."

Tee knew that he had a friend in need who truly needed him because he don't have nobody but him.

As he stepped into the house and took off his shoes and laid down, Tee began thinking of a way to help Tony out since it's about 8:30 p.m.

Tee and Jay had planned on going to the club, but he wanted to ride out to the east, so he said that it will be a pretty good crowd at Cactus Jack's and told Tee to "dress to impress."

Shay already left and went to her friend's party, so he decided to step out with his nigga Jay. He knew that they were going to get up with some hoes and he also knew that they were going to leave that joint with some freaks. So, he decided to get as fresh as he could in his Akoo outfit and Jordan's Six Rings Championship Shoes.

Jay pulled up in his two-door, drop-top '72 Cutlass and it was purple and black with gold O'Reilly stripes and had black inside guts. My homie had 24s on that joint, with a system that was out of this world because everything was customized. A super clean paint job that was like glass and sounded like drums beating from the system itself. Also, he had concert TVs in the headrest with customized doors that feature the lambo style.

We pulled off and headed towards the east to Cactus Jack's, and the line were all the way in the parking lot. It was like all eyes on us, and Jay let his top down as I let my door up and stood outside the car.

These two females pulled up right beside us and was eyeballing me, so I acted like I didn't see them, but Jay did, though.

"Damn, my nigga," Jay stated as Tee began to ignore the hoes in the Benz. Jay asked with authority, "Cuz, aren't you gone say something to them?"

"Hell, no, cuz, because all those hoes want to do is get in a nigga pockets," Tee replied.

Jay then stated, "come off of that shit, cuz." When he said that he threw Tee a fat bank roll so he could get his party on. So, Jay looked at him and stated, "Just play your cards right, cuz."

Tee said, "That isn't nothing but $50."

Jay said, "The ones make it look big, don't it, cuz?"

Ha! Ha! Ha!

By the time he turned around to the hoes he then said, "What's up, li'l mama?" to the driver.

"You!" She said, stepping out the car while she showed her legs off. They were big and sexy as ever, but Tee continued looking at what had him stunned. Tee seen that she had on nothing but booty shorts and tall boots cutting in between her legs showing her split.

By the time Jay walked up, Tee said, "Looks like to me that you got the better hand." Tee asked her, "What's your name?"

She said, "It's Princess. What's yours?"

Tee then replied, "Let me get your number and I will call you later, shawty, and then we can discuss all this on the phone."

She pulled out a pen and a piece of paper and wrote her number down and handed it to Tee. Jay walked off with her friend, heading to the VIP line, then Tee headed towards that way also.

Princess was still at her car doing something as Jay walked in and seen that it were jam packed from wall to wall. So, she asked, "Where Princess and Tee at?"

"Here we go, Jay," Tee stated.

Then they sat down right at the second table in the VIP and Princess and her friend invited themselves to sit with us.

"What's up with y'all?" Jay said, smiling at Princess' friend. She said she wanted to finish talking to his friend and she wanted to come with Princess.

"Y'all expecting company?" Princess asked happily.

"Not really," Jay said. "Ya'll cool."

"So, what you wanted to let me know, Baby Girl?" She specified, "I were feeling you and I wanted tonight to be our night."

Princess said, "I don't get out much and that's why I'd rather kick it with Tee tonight. Do you have anything planned, Tee?"

Then Tee stated, "Don't really have nothing going on, but just kicking it with my homie. But if your friend going to kick it with him, then we can chill."

She replied, "I guess we can do that then."

Jay said, "Y'all want to get a room?"

"Hold on a minute," Tee got up and told Jay to come with him.

"What's up, my nigga?" Jay said. "Man, that whore is ready, she's already talking about getting a room."

"Just her or her and her friend?" Tee asked.

Jay said, "I don't know, but I'm with it. How about you, Tee?"

Tee said, "Come on, my nigga, you know I'm with it. But we're gone chill and have some drinks first."

"Okay!"

So, they ordered drinks for Princess and Baby Girl and then they begin to let them know the business about the rest of the night. Tee walked back over to Princess and told her the business and she agreed, and her friend did too.

"Where are we going once we leave here?" they asked with excitement.

Tee and Jay said they are going to the Marriot in East Memphis off Perkins and American Way.

Jay said, "I'm about to get ready to go," as he drank the last of the New Amsterdam.

Tee stated, "Yeah, let's get the hell out of here because it's getting late."

As they left the club and headed to the Marriot, Princess and her friend remained for a minute and told Tee and Jay that they will meet them there as soon as they leave the club.

When they made it to the hotel and seen Princess and Baby Girl pulling up, Jay said, "I think that she's ready for this dick." So, they both walked to catch up with them as they went into the hotel.

While at the customer service desk they each got separate rooms. Tee and Princess got room 211 and Jay and Baby Girl got room 212. The first thing Tee did when him and Princess walked into the room was jump into the shower.

Afterwards, Tee made sure that his body was clean enough for her to put her lips on his dick and that she wouldn't taste any salt.

She came in the shower butt-ass naked and started sucking the shit out of Tee's dick. Soon as it got hard, she got all the way in the shower and put her hands on the wall.

When Tee stuck his hard dick into that juicy pussy, and it felt good to him as the steaming water ran down their backs. And man, this girl had one of the fattest asses you will ever see. Tee begin hitting it slow and she seem to enjoy every bit of that dick she were receiving from him.

Tee finally cum and both of them washed up and got in bed to finish the rest of the night making love. She asked him, "Did you like that, daddy?" laying in the bed rubbing his chest.

He said, "And you know it, li'l mama. What about you?"

She replied, "Baby, I heard bells, you put me in a spot I never experienced in my life."

And after she said that, Tee knew the Benz was his shit now.

Tee laid down and Princess did too as they fell asleep naked on top of the covers.

Tee was woken up by the bright sun the next morning, while Princess continue to lay there on the other side of the bed. She was still butt naked.

Tee said, "Since she hasn't put nothing on yet, might as well get ready for round two." Tee turned her over on her back and he entered inside of her, then she pulled him closer as she opened her eyes.

Princess grabbed him around his waist, pulling him to her breast, then she moaned in his ear. After that, she exhaled something that he wasn't looking for at all, "I love you, baby…"

Tee stated, "What the hell!" while he were stroking in and out of that tight, wet pussy. After they finished, he got up and put on his boxers as he went to look out the window to see if Jay and her friend was still out there.

Princess got in the shower and then he begin thinking about home and his woman Shay. He knew he had to come up with some kind of excuse or Shay was going to be mad as hell at him.

Ten minutes later Princess came walking out the shower, so she asked, "Do you got a woman at home?"

Tee replied, "Yeah, I do."

Then she said, "Damn, that's fucked up!"

Tee asked, "Why you say that?"

She stated, "Because I want a man of my own and not somebody to share with another bitch." Then she said, "I don't know at this moment, but I need some time to think about it. Don't get me wrong, because I do like you a lot, but you got a woman. So where do you stay at and what's your story?"

Tee said, "I think we need to talk about this later, sweetie, it's checkout time."

Princess and Tee walked out the room and went to Jay and Mica's room as they realized Jay and Mica were already coming out the door.

Jay had his arms around her, and she was smiling, looking in his face. I guess that's a sign that they had a hell of a good time last night.

"What's up, y'all?"

Princess said, "Shit, girl, you ready?" sounding really upset.

"Hold on," Mica stated vigorously. "Hold on, Princess, you're mad about something."

Princess replied, "Mad about what? I have no reason to be."

Tee pulled her to the side telling her to come here.

"Princess!" he called, then Jay and Mica walked to their cars.

"Look, Princess, before you make up ya mind that you're not going to mess with me anymore, give me a chance to see what's going to happen. We should start off as friends first before we jump right into this relationship thing. Don't you feel me, sexy?"

She said, "That sounds fair."

Tee said, "That's better, right?"

She shook her head up and down as she walked to her car, then she got in and reached in her pocket while standing beside Jay's car.

Tee still had her number, so that's good. He eventually got into his homeboy's car as he closed the door and looked at Jay.

As Jay looked at him, Tee stated, "What I say?" smiling at Jay. "I didn't say that shit."

Jay said, "Nigga, you shouldn't never told her you had a woman," while cranking up the car. He threw his arm around the seat and balled out. "So, old girl want to be the number one thing, huh?" Jay asked.

"I guess," Tee said.

"Mane!" Jay said. "Shay 'bout to kill you and yo ass fucked up, homie."

Tee said, "It's nothing."

After that Jay was like a quiet mouse on Halloween as they went on to their destination.

They pulled up at Tee's crib and got out the car, then walked into the house. It was a blessing that Shay weren't home, so he grabbed the phone to see if she's been calling this morning. He sat down for a minute as he tried to come up with the best lie he could tell. Once he could figure one out he just called her himself.

Tee waited as the phone rang. "Hello!" she stated. Then she asked him, "Where the hell have you been, baby?"

Tee replied, "I got drunk over Jay house and fell asleep on the couch. I know I didn't wake up to call you, okay."

"If that is what really happened," Shay replied. She then said, "But if I find out you lied to me it's over with, and I mean that 100 percent, Tee. You are getting a cell phone today when I get off of work."

Tee stated, "I don't want a phone."

"It's not for you, it's for me," she replied. Also, Shay told him that, "It's to keep up with your ass because I'm not about to go through this shit with you, baby. We will have to talk when I get home, baby."

"Okay, baby."

"Okay."

Tee thought shit is going okay and I'm in the clear so far, but I know that she is mad as hell, though. Tee did well because he still had some money from what Jay game him last night.

Tee went to Tony's mother's house and when he arrived at her house he knocked on the door, knock, knock knock! Nobody came to the door. Therefore, he walked back to his crib and there was nothing he wanted to do now. So, he laid down on the couch and thought for a minute about how he could help this nigga get out of jail, especially if he didn't do it. Tony don't have no help and he believe that they planted this shit on him. Tee had a plan but couldn't tell a soul about it.

"It's gone have to take some time to put this shit together now, so that's what I'll do for me and for my homie Tony Talley." Tee thought to himself if he just had a way to help it'll be alright for Tony, then he will be more loyal to him for helping him in this situation.

Tee gathered up some funds and told Jay he is about to try to get this lawyer for Tony as well as get him out on bond. This was the best thing that Tee could have come up with over the last few days, and with all the things he have done for Tony, he still feel obligated to help his homie.

Tee was a real homeboy and he didn't lie to them about anything he was gone do for his homeboys. This was the first time seeing a real man do what he said he were gone do for his homies.

Tony called Tee from jail and Tee accepted the phone call. "Hello, nigga! What's crackin' with ya, homie?" Tony asked.

Tee stated, "I'm as happy to hear from you, cuz, as always. I am trying to get an attorney to help you on your case, homeboy."

Tony said, "Thanks, homie!"

Tee told him, "I'll put some money on your book when I come visit today, as well."

Tee then hung up the phone and started getting dressed so he can start his day off. Once he decided to leave the crib he headed to go see his homie as well as put money on his books.

Tee arrived at 201 Poplar Avenue and entered the jail to see Tony, and when he made it to the window he put $50 on his books, then he went to see his friend.

While visiting him he told Tony to be cool because he were working to get him out of jail.

Tee have been to 201 Poplar two more times to see Tony since nobody else have, so he made it his business to do it. The money Tony have been getting has been from Tee, and since they let his girl go yesterday.

Tee said, "You'll be out in a minute. Once I leave I go over to Memphis Bonding Company to holler at Calvin about posting your bond for you."

Tee were so real to the hood that he took risks that no other homies took for the hood.

Hopefully, he can help with everything he need because he got a court date, especially help to find a lawyer to represent him because it's two weeks from today until Tony have to be in court.

Tee stated, "I got to make a move sooner than I thought I was, homie." Tee never did get a chance to talk to Tony's mother, and when he seen her, he tried to tell her about what he said, but she ignored Tee. She started walking away from Tee as he tried talking to her about Tony with his case.

CHAPTER 4

However, Tee have been talking to Princess, and she start telling him how she miss the shit out of him.

Tee lied to her about him and his girl being on bad terms and that they may end up together, which neither one of them knows the truth to that nor is he ready to let her go yet because everybody needs a backup plan.

Tee walked to the store and by coincidence he seen Princess. As a result, he stepped out of Mapco to speak to her while she was pumping gas.

He stated, "What's up, baby?"

"Nothing, but what's up with you?"

"Well, I had no choice but to step to you because you're looking so damn good, and I mean so good that I want to make you my lunch."

"Well, I know that you have your girl." Then she said, "I will continue to be cool with you. On the other hand, I'm just getting off work and I'm on my way to the crib, so call me later if you're cool with that, Tee. What you're about to do now, if you don't mind me asking?"

Princess put her hands on her hips, and she looked him up and down as she were walking inside the store. He then walked behind her, admiring her phat ass and the way she stepped when she walked.

"What?" she replied.

"Is it something I said, baby?"

"Naw. Just knowing you don't give a damn about me enough to be with me because my friend and I was just a good time to you and your homeboy."

Tee replied, "No, I wanted to be with you for real, but I didn't know if you was ready to be mine, Princess."

While in the store she told the cashier, "$10 on three, please." Then she told Tee, "Nigga, please!" then she walked out the door.

Princess said, "I'll see if one of us made progress, Tee. On top of that, Tee, you barely call me, so what am I supposed to think? I'm not no hoe by a long shot, nigga." She then told him she wanted to be loved and she needed a thug in her life that's true to her as well as himself.

So, he asked, "You really want me?"

She replied, "Should I?"

Then Tee stated, "You should."

After that she put her gas cap back on and hung up the pump. Then she headed to the driver's side door of her purple 2009 Lexus LS 400 coupe. Tee walked up to the door with her as he asked her again, "Do you really want to be with me?"

She stated, "What the hell do you think, nigga?"

When he heard that, he seen a tear fall from her eye, then he knew she was for real.

Tee stepped from the car as she closed the door, then he pecked on the window. She let the window down and he told her, "I'm going to call you tonight."

Princess wiped her eyes from the tears that ran down her face and she pulled off as she waved goodbye to Tee. Then Tee walked to his crib.

When he called Princess he told her that he was gone have his clothes ready and they were gone see how things work out.

"Don't play with me, Tee. I didn't asked to be lied to neither," Princess stated to Tee.

"I'm not," he said, then hung up the phone. Tee walked to the house and sat down on the steps thinking about life itself.

"Why are you just sitting out here for, baby?" Shay asked.

He replied, "I don't know," as he turned around looking at Shay.

She asked, "Can I sit out here with you?"

He stated, "I don't care," as she came out to sit down beside him.

"What's the matter?" she asked.

He replied, "Confused as hell."

She asked, "About what?"

Tee told Shay, "It's the world, people, and everything. You know how it is when you get tired."

Shay asked, "Is it something I did?"

When she stated that he just looked at her because she really was concerned about what was going on with him.

"No, baby, you haven't done anything! You know, it's fucked up when you go to jail for something you haven't even done. I don't believe nobody deserves to go to jail if they didn't do shit."

"You talking about Tory, baby?"

"Anybody! It's not right and I have done all I can do. Now I can't do anything else, baby. Tony is a good person, and nobody has tried or is even trying to help him out but me. His mother don't even visit him or put money on his books, baby."

Shay put her arms around Tee and leaned in on his chest and said, "I know what you mean. I know you hate to see people do people wrong, but baby, you're a good person too. I know that for a fact, Tee. Baby, believe it or not, I've learned so much from you, babe," Shay said passionately. "I know whatever is bothering you you're going to fix it 100 percent. I know that you do a lot of thinking for good reasons, baby. You keep me motivated, but sometimes you give up, though," Shay said meaningfully. "Then you start to make stupid decisions, and that is what really pisses me off, baby."

When she said that, two headlights pulled up in the front of Tee's house, so he stood up trying to see who it was that were driving, but it was dark as hell. Suddenly, the driver side door opened and Jay stepped out.

"Oh, shit! What's up, cuz?"

Shay got up and walked in the house because she knew he didn't play that hanging around them while he and his homie talked unless his girl were with him. The reason was Tee didn't want females in their business.

"Not shit!" Jay replied instantly. Jay said that he came to holler at me on some business-type of shit and if I'm down for it. Then Jay said," Come on, let's sit in the car and talk about the business, homeboy."

Jay and Tee walked back to the car and they both got in at the same time, so as he talked, Tee listened because he was talking big talk, which were Tee kind of talk.

Jay said, "I have a move on some niggas that can get us paid," and he asked Tee, "You with that 100 percent?"

Tee stated, "Nigga, you better know it. I can get Tony out,

move out the hood, and live a better life than the one I've been living."

He was going to give Tee everything he need to make all this come to play, and knowing that it's all for the cause, Tee said, "I'm down!"

Jay needed me to pay close attention and don't miss a bit because one mistake can cost me my life.

Tee said, "I'm not going with anyone because I have to do this alone."

"Any questions?" Jay asked.

"Not at the moment, cuz," Tee said

Then Jay asked him, "Can you handle it?"

"There is only one way to find that out, isn't it?" Tee replied.

Jay said to him, as he looked at Tee for the first time, "Okay, I'll be back to bring you the car with everything else you're gone need."

"This car must be hot?"

Jay answered, "It's just a rental."

"Okay, then," Tee said while opening up the door to get out the car.

He closed the door and walked into the apartment complex and then he walked into his apartment.

"Now what?" Shay said angrily.

"What are you talking about?" Tee replied.

She said, "What did he want with you, babe?"

"He just told me he was going out of town and asked me would I come by tonight to keep an eye on his spot for him."

"What did you say?" she asked.

"I told him I would, besides, he is paying me, so what is the fuckin' problem, baby? It isn't like I got something to do," he said to Shay.

"Baby, what if the police decides to kick in his door while you got your dumb ass in there asleep?" she replied.

"Baby, it won't be any drugs or guns in there, and if that's true, they can't charge me with nothing." Tee told her that to make up the biggest lie he ever told and make it sound so true.

Shay told him, "Fuck it! That's you. Go on, go, because if you go to jail it's on you, baby, and you do have a choice. If you go to jail, what choice will you have then, Tee? Baby, you're taking a risk of leaving me out here on my own and that's gone make things worse."

Tee couldn't say nothing else because he knew it was what it was and that were the final answer coming from Shay.

Tee called her name, "Shay, baby."

"What the hell do you want, nigga?" Shay stated as she slammed the bedroom door.

Tee said, "I want to talk, sweetie." Then he went set down at the kitchen table and fired up a Newport. He sat back to relax his nerves before he go on that mission. He laughed to himself, "mission," and that is when he thought about 007 and replied, "Life is a trip, isn't it?"

CHAPTER 5

Here's the keys to the car. You know how to work this, right?" while passing me a 9mm with the extended clip. Tee stated, "What you think?" and smirked. "What's this for?" Tee asked, looking at a funny-shaped object that was shaped like a glass cutter.

"That's not for you, Tee, it's used to crack safes," Jay stated. Then he asked, "Do you want that job instead?" while looking real as hell.

Tee replied, "I'm okay," then he headed out the door so he could get on with the job at hand. He jumped into the car and cranked it up then put it in drive and drove to the spot.

He pulled up to an empty house four houses down the street and sat there until the car that were supposed to leave left. Tee put on his black latex gloves and went behind the empty house.

It was an Army green box with a lock on it and the key that he got from Jay.

So, Tee opened the box and got the small night vision glasses, the vest, and also, a black mask that covers everything but his eyes. He was ready to achieve his mission as he went through the back door of that abandoned house then jumped all the fences that were in people back yards.

He finally made it to the last fence, but first he had to make sure that everything was good. He took the night vision x-ray glasses off his head on to his eyes and he stood on a crate that was by the fence, then looked at the house as well as the back yard. If somebody was around it would've showed because it's supposed to be only one person like Jay said, which is supposed to be a woman. Tee went on to jump the fence and then walked up to the back door.

Tee had the keys to the door, and he opened the door to the kitchen, and everything were in the right place as Jay told him it's gone be. So, he crept up into the living room next and then the bedroom. He was supposed to tie her up and not let her get out the house until he's finally out of the area.

He waited around until the bed lights went off, and that's when he sneaked in and made his move. He grabbed her as soon as she showed herself. Tee were right on it step by step as he crawled on the floor. He got close enough to the bed then took out the gun as he took a deep breath and stood up. "Here goes nothing," he thought, "and here goes his fourth time robbing somebody."

The first thing he did was mask up and mask her to take out her eyesight. After that, he held down all the screaming from the mask. The next thing he did was wrapped the rope around her hands and legs, then he watched her for a brief moment. Now he's able to see what he's doing because of the light from the TV.

"Okay, we can do this the easy way or we can do this the hard way," Tee stated. "You know what I want and if I don't get it, you isn't going to be happy."

Clock! Clock! "I don't know what you want from me," she said, coughing.

Tee pulled a lot of strings to get to this point and now he's at that point. Consequently, he said arguably, "I need the money and the dope."

After that she kept coughing and gagging out the mouth and then she pointed to the closet. "Right there."

Tee then said, "There?" pointing to the closet with the gun, and she shook her head up and down. So, he opened up the closet door and seen a small secret door in the bottom of the closet wall. He opened it up and it was a safe there. "Damn," he stated because nobody said shit 'bout this.

"What's the number to this fucking thing?" he said, getting upset.

"I don't know the number, he never tell it to me," she said sincerely.

She was done choking from the mask, but her eyes was closed. Tee had to come up with something fast, so he walked around in circles for a little minute as he came up with a master plan of his own.

First, he took a knife and put it to the mix bitch throat. "Look, bitch, I told you what I came for and what is going to happen if I don't get it."

She started crying as tears were already coming from her eyes from the mask, then more tears started coming as she begin begging, "Please don't hurt me. He just got that put in today," she said honestly.

Tee wasn't gone kill her anyway, but he had to make it look good. Only one thing left to do, which is to pull it out the wall. Tee worked hard with it until he were able to get that heavy safe out the fuckin' wall because it were every bit of 200 pounds.

Now the hard part is getting out, and fortunate for him it wasn't bolted down. So, he picked it up and tried to think of a way he could get this safe out of the house. He walked to the front door and looked out the window first, and even though he didn't want to go that way, it was a reason that Jay wanted him to park down the street as well as go through them back yards and shit. Besides, shit had changed as he wasn't about to give up after he got all this done.

He ran out the back door and jumped over all the fences until he made it to the car. He then drove it to the house with the lights off as he pulled in the driveway to the back yard. Afterwards, Tee walked back into the house as he went to the bedroom and seen her struggling to get loose. He picked up the safe and struggled with it all the way to the trunk of the car and then put it inside. "Wish this nigga would have told me about this damn safe at the beginning. Hell!"

Tee then pulled up at the house Jay told him to pull up at, hit the horn two times like he were told to do, then the garage doors opened as two females walked out and came up to the car.

"You must be Tee," a tall, slim girl stated with some short shorts on replied.

"Yeah, what you think?" Tee stated, mad at Jay. "Where Jay at?" he asked her.

She stated, "What's ya problem, baby?"

He replied, "Baby, I don't have a problem. Who do you supposed to be, baby?"

"I'm Jay's sister."

"Pull the car in the garage," the other one said, "and if you want, I'll call Jay so you can talk to him."

Tee pull the car in the garage, and he got out as she handed him the phone. He snatched the phone from her and put it to his ear as he said, "Hello," Jay said on the other end.

"Man, we got two problems."

"What's that, homie?"

"First of all, the shit didn't go exactly as I planned it. I personally wasn't going to make a blank mission either."

Jay asked, "What's wrong, Tee?"

"What happened?" Tee replied. "Man, who is these folks in the garage? It's two females and they can see my face. You said a nigga was going to be here."

"They're good, Tee. One thing I will never do is cross somebody I fuck with because all I have is my balls and my word," Jay replied. "I just told you they straight. Now if you don't feel the scene and want to leave, just let me know and you can do so," Jay stated.

"I'm good, but it was a safe instead of money and dope, so I had to pull the car in the driveway to get it."

"Did anybody follow you?" Jay asked nervously.

Tee replied, "Didn't nobody followed me, cuz. We good on that."

"Okay." Jay told Tee, "The tall one is in control, her name is Tasha, that's my sister. Her friend with the shit too so you all stay calm until I get over there, and try to open the safe."

"I got ya, homie, it isn't no turning back."

With that said, Jay hung the phone up. Tee knew just what he meant. He gave the phone back to Tasha and opened the trunk.

"We need to get t his opened," he stated to the beautiful women. "How we gone do that?" the short one asked.

Tee replied, "I don't know, but we put our heads together, we can get it opened."

"Why we need to open it?"

"Jay told me to. What did my brother say?" Tee said. "Try to open the safe."

"Don't he have one of them things with the pump on it at the house for shit like this?"

"Oh, yeah!" Tee said in shock. He had forgot about that 'cause all of the excitement that's going on. So, all we got to do is wait until he get here, right?

Then Tasha and the other girl looked at each other and said, "I guess so, if he got that thing we need," shawty stated.

Jay pulled up and then Tee knew it was him because how the doors on his car closed. We all was in the house talking in the dining room. Tasha seen Tee getting freaky with the sort one, and Jay got out the car with the pump in his hands ready to crack open this safe.

Tasha opened the garage door as we all walked in and the short girl closed it behind us. We opened the trunk, and since Jay was the only person knew how to work the safe opener, he had to do it.

He slid the pump in the spot it were supposed to go and started pumping the pump. Finally, the safe opened up and it was full of money.

"Damn," Tee said to himself. He was the only person looking like he never ever seen that much money before. He paid so much attention to that money as he got himself together.

"That nigga must don't have the dope no more," Jay said, "or he put it in another spot. Well, let's see what we got. Anybody got a bag? Go get that bag over there, shorty," he said to the little one.

She walked in the corner where Jay pointed and got the bag and handed it to Jay. Jay filled the bag up as we all walked in the house to get our cut. It was like $175,000 in that safe, and I don't know what everybody else got, but I got $85,000 out of the lick. That's almost half of it, so I was happy.

Tee and Jay rode home together. The girls was supposed to get rid of the safe and take the car back to where it belong to. Afterwards, we pulled up at Jay's house and Tee thought about the Princess bitch sitting in the car. We both had too much money on us to just be sitting out here this way and I was not used to it, but I didn't know about him.

"So, what are you going to do with all that you have, Tee?" Jay asked.

Tee told Jay "You know, I got to help my nigga out," he said happily.

Jay said, "That's what's up, cuz."

"Well," Tee stated, "let me get to the house 'cause I got a lot of shit to be done." On his way to the house he stopped and knocked on Tony's girl's door because he knew if she was not up she had to be at home.

He knocked on the door and knocking turned into banging on the door, then she opened it. "Damn, Tee! What's all that about?" she said in the door with her sleepers on.

Tee replied, "It's about Tony. How do you know my name? Well, so much for an introduction, I need to talk to you."

"Okay."

"Talk," she said. Tee looked around like somebody was watching him and then asked, "Can I come in, baby girl?"

She put a funny look on her face and then she said, "It's about Tony? Come on in, nigga."

So, Tee walked in the house and seen that it was fucked up. Big-ass roaches everywhere, dirty clothes all over the floor, and the smell made him wish he would have stayed outside on the porch because it were past funky.

"What is it?" Stephanie asked in a sassy voice.

Tee asked, "How much can you come up with to get a lawyer or whatever we need to beat this case, Stephanie, because I don't believe Tony did shit."

"Tee, baby, I'm barely making it and I'm on Section 8. I can't even pay my damn bills," she replied instantly. "How you figure he didn't do it, anyway, Tee?"

"What? You think he did this shit, Stephanie?" Tee said to her in amazement.

"Sweetie, I don't know, but he was acting funny the night we hooked up, and that's why I said that, Tee. So, why are you asking what I can come up with? What have you got, Tee?"

Tee said, "What I need to have, Stephanie?"

"Tony called today and told me he knew a lawyer that can get him off for $2,000."

"Two thousand dollars!" Tee replied.

That's when Stephanie shook her head up and down, so Tee reached in his bag that had the 85 Gs and pulled out one stack of hundred dollar bills.

"Boy! Where did you get all this money?" Stephanie asked.

Tee stated, "Don't worry about that, you ain't seen shit," Tee said happily.

"Okay."

"Don't even tell Tony. Just get him out and tell him I put in a little help." Tee gave her the 2 Gs and she said, "Thank you!" then she walked out the door.

Tee walked home feeling like he did something good today. So, when he made it home he looked at his car and knew what he needed to do about all his problems, he thought honestly.

CHAPTER 6

Tee set in the house three whole days waiting to see if he could hear something from the streets. Since the streets wasn't talking, Tee decided to pop the hood of his car and check it. After seeing that his motor was intact he went and checked out Shay's car. He didn't tell her nothing about the other night, but she knew something wasn't right, and she wasn't gone find out either because he got her a 2001 Mustang even though he don't like them because he don't do Fords, but it's what she wanted.

Tee didn't worry about it at all 'cause he had to drive her to work today, so they rolled in her car, and because he were still laying low from all the things he done four nights ago.

Tee drove Shay car until it was time to go pick her up from work. Now it's his turn to go celebrate our anniversary, and he was going to do it big. Just what he was looking for.

As he entered the mall jewelry store he seen a three-karat diamond ring with princess cuts and were made for a princess. Tee snatched the ring and drove to the car lot where he seen a 1976 Chevy drop-top hard body. It was dark blue with a solid white top and the motor and frame was good. He got the keys to test drive it and put a down payment on it.

He pulled up at a paint shop to find out what paint job he wanted to get and how much they charge for that paint job. It was two-and-a-half Gs for a candy purple with royal gloss. Tee went and bought some 26-inch rims and tires for six-and-a-half Gs. Along with that he bought a system that sounded like an earthquake because it were a package deal that totaled nine Gs.

Afterwards, he went got him a pizza and salad 'cause he was hungry as hell. While he was at Pizza hut he called Princess to talk to her about hooking up later on.

Princess said, "Maybe, if it's gone be for real, 'cause last time you stood me up."

That's when he told her something came up very important he had to take care of it.

Princess stated, "Nigga, you act like you scared of this pussy. You're always running every time I want to hook up with you to fulfill your needs."

Tee then said, "It's not that at all, cuz, it's money over bitches any day of the week."

Princess said sarcastically, "Bitches get paid and niggas get played."

Tee replied, "Bitches aren't shit but a tool for a pimp like me." Then he stated, "I'm the Don of all Dons and I'll make you be who I want you to be fuckin' with me, Princess. Therefore, you better know it for ya blow it, babe, 'cause I'm the prize, not you, bitch. Get with it or get shitted on because it's your choice."

Tee went on, "Whores gone be whores with a pimp or without a pimp."

As he hung up the phone he left Pizza Hut and went over Jay's house. When he got there he had a house full of niggas. Tee walked in and began to look for Jay, and when Jay saw him he stated, "You just the nigga I need to see," as Tee sat on the couch in the living room.

He snatched Tee up off the couch and told him that he fucked up. Tee seen about five niggas sitting around a glass table with AK-47s everywhere.

Jay had Tee pinned up against the wall with his fist. "What's up, cuz?" Tee replied, trying to figure out what is going on and what's fucking wrong with Jay.

Jay replied, "Tee, you fucked up, man, you didn't do it right, my nigga."

"What? What do you mean? What I didn't do right?" he said, sounding so damn confused. He really thought deeply in his heart that he didn't fuck up because Jay never complained about the missions Tee pulled off before this one.

That's when Jay said, "You didn't make it seem like somebody broke in the house. The young nigga all over the hood throwing shit in the air, so you need to get one of these guns and go handle that, cuz. We can't be having niggas hunting for our heads 'cause the mission wasn't done properly, ya dig?"

Tee told Jay that it'll be taken care of on his time because proper preparation prevents poor performance. Then he said, "Stop acting like a scary-ass sucker," Tee said ferociously to Jay.

Jay said, "I got ya, homie. That's what's up, cuz. Anyway, I know you need to get one of these guns."

Tee said, I am as I get a chance, cuz."

"I'm going to show you who this dude is," Jay said smirking. "Tee, you need to be careful and check on me every day. I'm mad at you, but fuck it, we together, so get ready. I don't know when, but the day is going to come and shit isn't gone be pretty."

"I gotcha, cuz, and that's my bad, though," Tee replied.

"Don't worry about it, we got to fix it, too late to cry. That's what's up," Jay replied, and then he stated, "It's about time to get gangsta." Jay told Tee to take the same gun with him from the night before. "It's yours, so keep up with it and don't ever let nobody know what you got, Tee, rather it's money, guns, or your next move, okay?"

"I gotcha, cuz," Tee replied with a frown on his face because Jay acting like he's dumb and I'm for real 'cause it is a reason why I'm telling you this, cuz.

"I'm going to teach you the whole thing," Jay said.

"That's what's up, cuz," Tee stated.

Afterwards, Jay filled Tee in on the plan and Tee walked towards the door with Jay. When they made it to the door he stopped and told him to be careful.

Tee told Jay he would as he got into his girl's car. Tee would make sure he's very cautious riding these streets. There sure as hell isn't any way out now. Then he drove to the Cricket store on Winchester and Hack Cross by Kroger to get another phone. On top of that, he got the cheapest phone they had in the display. The bill was $50 a month with unlimited text and data. Once he got the phone he called Shay, then he called Jay, then he called Princess.

"Hello?" she said over the phone.

Tee said, "What's up?"

She stated, "What's up? Who is this?"

"This is Tee," he replied.

"Man, please, don't call me no more," she said and hung up the phone. Tee called back and the answering machine came on, so he left a message. "What's up, gorgeous? I know that you're upset and you've got every right to be, but look, I need to talk to you whenever you feel up to it. When you get this message call this number, okay?" With that said, he hung up the phone.

Tee got on I-240 on his way to pick up Shay from the workplace and the traffic was super thick. He happened to look in the rearview mirror as he seen a police car behind him. Then his heart started beating really fast. Tee kept himself afloat and he checked to make sure he wasn't speeding. When he realized his seatbelt wasn't on he knew that he's gone for sure.

Tee tried to sneak it on so that he could snap it up, and as soon as the Suburban beside him got over the police hit his lights and Tee's heart was about to jump out of his chest. The first thing he were about to do was roll down the window then throw the gun out the window. However, as soon as he started to get over, the police drove straight past him. He took a deep, deep breath and fired up a cigarette. As soon as he took the first puff it were truly a relief.

The first thing came to his mind was where to pull over and put that damn gun up? He can't get caught with this damn pistol, so he got off at the Parkway exit from the expressway.

Meanwhile, he turned around in the car and seen a pregnancy test in the floor of the back seat. He picked up the li'l thermal strike and seen a plus sign on it, but he decided that he need to wait to see if she's going to tell him herself.

Tee made a stop at his brother's house and went into the house to place the gun he had under the mattress in the bedroom. Tee paid attention to the time on the phone so that he wouldn't be late, but he was late, so Shay asked, "Why you're late pulling up?"

Tee replied, "Baby, I had to make a stop at the house to take a shit."

"Okay."

"Baby, I'm ready, though."

"Okay."

Tee thought, "Today has been one heck of a day, and once I get back to the crib I'm going to relax with my baby, Shay Harris."

Shay walked around the car and told Tee to get on the passenger side because she's driving. She hit the first gear and sped off. "Shit, you don't even like Fords. Let me show you what this thing can do, handsome," Shay said to Tee.

"Whatever!" Tee said, snapping on his seatbelt as Shay hit the gas. She thought she were in a Nascar race on the expressway as we passed several cars and trucks.

Tee then said to her, "Girl, you think this thing is the truth?"

She said, "I know it is because my dad used to have one."

Tee said in amazement, "So that's why ya wanted one?"

"No, I just like them because they're fast," Shay replied.

So, he said that it can't fuck with what he's got, and she stated, "That broke down Chevy?"

Tee told her that he got another Chevy today and that joint is super ready.

"Yeah!" Shay said, pushing the gas while pulling off at the light. "Don't pull up beside my shit," she replied. Then she stated, "A Chevy can't come close to a Stang…short for Mustang."

As he laid back and enjoyed the way she showed him about her car, they pulled up at the apartments and Tee seen Tony sitting down on the sidewalk and it were over old girl's house.

"Tony!" he said, hollering for him to come over. So, tony got up and walked up to Tee. He stuck his hand out for him to shake it and they hands connected. Tee snatched Tony to him and gave him a big, strong hug.

"Thanks, man! You've been like a father to me, Tee."

"Really, man?"

"I really mean it."

"Hey, man, say man," Tee was trying not to get too emotional.

"Okay, cuz, but you can let me go now, homie."

Tony stepped back and gave Tee that size-up look. "Look at ya, homie, ya on ya shine, huh?" Tony said, looking at his new clothes he had on.

"Oooow!"

"Who whip is this?" pointing at Shay's car.

"Oh," Tee told him, "That's my baby's junt, nigga. You like that, don't ya?" Tee said to Tony.

Tony stated, "Hell, yeah, 'cause that's the Shelby GT 500 joint," Tony replied.

Tee told him that he didn't know because he don't do Fords.

"What do you have against a Ford?" Tony asked.

Tee replied, "Just not my style."

"So, what's going on, cuz?" Tony asked.

Tee said, "Enough of the small talk, you owe me, homie." After that, Tony held his head down.

Tony stated, "I know I owe you big time, and what is it that I can do for you, homie?"

Tee then said, "I'll let ya know when the time is right. But for now, just keep being Tony, the crazy homeboy from the hood that fuck with Tee. It's on from here on out. And by the way, I got something for you to do," Tee said.

Tony replied, "What's that, cuz?"

Tee replied, "Take your ass home and stay out of trouble for me, okay?"

"I gotcha, cuz," Tony said as he shook Tee's hand and headed on down the sidewalk.

Tee watched him leave and he was like his child now. Tee walked into the crib and Shay were standing up in the kitchen looking out the back window.

"What are you looking, at, baby?"

Tee walked up to her smiling so hard, and she answered,

"Nothing but the kids in the park."

He said excitedly, "They look so happy out there in that park playing. Look at them, baby."

"Ain't they beautiful?" Shay said to Tee while he looked out the window at them. He already knew where she was coming from with this, but he was not going to say or the one to say it. Maybe she wanted it to be a surprise, and just maybe she wanted me to wait until she's ready or really know before she got my hopes up. Who knows?

Whatever it is, I know it will have led us to the bedroom. I love Shay, and I know that she loves me, and no one can tell me anything different. We laid down and watch a movie.

"What movie ya want to watch?" Tee asked.

Shay said, "Brothers," so Tee got up and went to get the bootlegged DVD case and put in "Brothers."

Tee asked her, "What do you think it is that I put in?"

She said, "It's either 'Life,' 'Hancock,' or 'Love Jones.'"

"Yeah, it's one out of the three," Tee replied.

"Well, what is it, baby?" Shay asked while laying on Tee's chest.

Shay started tickling Tee under his armpits and Tee told her to stop. She said, "Baby, you're getting mad about me tickling you?"

"No, you just got to wait until the movie comes on, li'l mama."

"You so wrong!" Shay said, frowning. After a few minutes she jumped up and hit him hard as hell on his chest.

"What's that all about?" Tee asked. He had forgot about the fact that they was waiting on the previews to go off and for the movie to come on.

"You said that it wasn't 'Life.'" Shay said.

"Did I say all that, baby?"

She shook her head up and down as we laid there enjoying the movie until we fell asleep.

CHAPTER 7

"Now that's what you call clean," Tony said while looking under the hood of Tee's 1976 Chevy Chevelle. "Look at the paint job. Candy purple with pearl flakes and triple gold deep dish Dayton's."

Tony was so enthusiastic about Tee's car that Tee told him, "Let's go for a spin."

"Say, man, this joint is super clean, cuz," Tony replied.

Then Tee replied, "It's okay, it ain't what I really wanted it to be, but it's straight."

They drove off, so Tee started to bump the system in his car, and then he put in that Tupac Shakur "All Eyes on Me" CD. While they were cruising on the e-way listening to the music the system sounded so good.

Tee pulled up at the store and some females pulled up beside them, and the females were smiling and cheesing at them. Tony were trying to play hard and shit, so Tee got out the car and he went into the store to buy him some Newport 100s and two coolers. Then one of them stated, "What's up witcha, handsome?" when they walked into the store.

The one had a Lakers jersey skirt and some Jordans to match, therefore, all eyes went on her instantly as she walked to the cooler to get a beer.

"Damn!" Tee replied. "That bitch is bad," and he walked out the store. He seen Tony talking to one of her friends, so he set there smoking a cigarette.

Tee began to look at the future of his life and realized that this street shit isn't really it, envisioning about what his future would turn out to be.

She walked out the store and approached him with a card that had her name and number on it and told Tee to call her later.

Tee was like, "Damn! For real, gorgeous?"

She said, "Let's create an empire, if that's cool with you, handsome."

Tee said, "Okay," and after that Tony got her friend's info before they pulled off. Tee and Tony then headed to East Memphis, and as Tee were about to get off at the Winchester exit his phone started ringing.

"Hello," he answered.

"What's up, nigga?" Princess asked. "So, you shining too good to say hi or even try to call me?"

Tee then replied, "I told you to call me whenever you got your spot."

"Look in ya mirror, Tee." So, he looked in his rearview mirror and seen Princess.

Tee pulled off to pull up at the store that were next to the liquor store on Knight Street and he hung up the phone as he got out the car. "What, you watching me or something?" Tee asked.

Then she said, "Why would I do that, Tee?"

Tee stated, "Because you're bugging me like you own me or something, bitch."

"Anyway, who car is this?" Princess asked.

"I just got this yesterday, babe," he said while she were checking it out.

Then she stated, "Why remain talking to you, anyway, because you don't want shit, especially me."

Tee told her it isn't like that because, "I really like ya, but it's just that we just met awhile ago. I got a woman that I just found out is pregnant, okay?"

Then Princess said, "I understand what you are saying," as she walked off and got into her car, and Tee did the same.

"Man!"

"Who is that bitch?" Tony asked as he walked out the liquor store.

Tee said, "That was Princess."

Tony then said, "Not her, but this bitch."

So, Tee looked at who he were talking about and said, "That's the bitch I robbed the other night," as she walked right in front of him.

Tee was in a daze while Tony was talking, but his words was sounding like clouds in Tee's ears. So, after a minute of being dazed out he heard him again.

"Tee! Tee! Ah, nigga, snap out of it."

"Oh, damn, what's up, cuz?"

"Nigga, what's wrong? You need to go to a doctor or something. Let me know, my nigga." Then he shook his head and they pulled off.

Now that we made it back to Tee's crib Shay and Keisha was in the house playing spades for money. Tee asked Tony if he was ready to kick their asses. Tony replied, "Let's get next. Hell, yeah."

Tee replied, "The game is on now!"

Shay and Keisha just won their game, so Tee and Tony sat down to play them a game of spades and they made a little wager with them for the night.

"What you got, Tony?" Tee asked, grinning.

"I got four on it, cuz," Tony replied.

"I got two, homie. We will go six and try to set them, cuz."

"Even though Shay and Keisha won the last two games, they will not win no more games," Tee said with confidence. He told Tony that they have to get a win under their belt because Shay and Keisha is kicking their butts. So, they played another game and finally won one.

Now that Tony and Tee won a game they said that they're through playing cards. "I'm tired of playing too," Shay said. "So, what you'll do about it?" Shay asked Keisha.

"We're about to roll out," Keisha said, referring to Tony.

"Yeah," Tony replied.

"Well, Shay, I'm going on to the house, girl," Keisha said. "I'll call you when I make it home, girl, because Tony and I have some unfinished business, if you know what I mean."

Tee sat on the steps as Shay went into the house, and Tee rolled up a blunt then fired it up. Tee smoked it by himself as he thought about Princess and remembered how good her pussy was to him. Just when he was about to go into the house to lay down his cellphone rang as it lit up like a tree, so he looked at his phone to see what number that were calling him as Shay looked at him.

"Baby, who is that?" she asked.

"Damn!" Tee whispered to himself, and then replied, "It was Jay, babe."

"What did you say?"

"It's Jay," he said angrily to her.

He answered the phone and said, "What's up, cuz?"

"Shit, nigga, come outside right fast," Jay said.

"Okay. Let me put some clothes on and I'll be out there, homie," and then he hung up the phone. Tee put his clothes on and told Shay that he doesn't think he's going anywhere.

Shay said, "I hope not," then stated, "You're constantly leaving me alone every single night and I'm getting tired of it, Tee. Keep that stuff up and I am going to do ya like that too," Shay said. Then she said it again as she turned over, covering her head up from being mad.

As Tee were standing in the bathroom door he walked into the living room door and then walked out the house to the front porch.

Jay then replied, "Nigga. what the hell did you do to the work, cuz?" as he were walking towards his car.

Tee hopped in the car and said, "Nigga, it's in a safe place, so stop tripping all the time, homie." Then Tee asked, "What's that business, cuz?"

Jay replied, "I need ya tomorrow night."

"What's going on?" Tee asked with curiosity.

"Shit! Get in and I will tell you what's going on, Tee. That's what's up, homie."

Tee said to Jay, "I see you have upgraded your whip," as he reached to open the door because it didn't have a handle on the door panel. That's when the door opened by itself and closed the same way. Even though when he got into the car and seen how the door was coming down on its own, he was stunned.

"Damn, nigga! You really upgraded, huh?" Tee asked.

"Ya know a gangsta got to do what he do, homie."

"Dig that shit," Tee said easily. "Anyway, what's the scoop, cuz?

"My nigga told me that the nigga moved out of his old house in the East somewhere."

"Word."

"Is that the nigga that want my head?"

"Yeah, that's the dude that want ya head, cuz."

"We got to find dude tomorrow night 'cause he's after me, homie. That's what's up."

"Oh, shit!" Tee stated. "I seen that bitch yesterday in da East."

"Straight up, cuz?" Jay asked.

"Straight up, homeboy," Tee replied. "That's for real, cuz, and that bitch were going in the store right by Knight Street, and ya know the liquor store is next to it."

"Did she see ya?" Jay asked.

"Naw, she walked right in front of my car. If she did see me, she still didn't know my face, homie."

"Yeah, that is true, cuz, because I know that you was masked up."

Tee replied, "You better know it, nigga.

"Well, nigga, just be ready tomorrow around 10:30 p.m., homie. By the way, how is that nigga Tony doing because I heard that he's out on bond.?"

"Yeah, that nigga is out on bond. I got him a lawyer and the lawyer got him out by getting the judge to lower his bond so Stephanie could get him out," Tee stated happily to Jay.

CHAPTER 8

It was about 9 p.m. and Tee just got to the house where the nigga live in the east and Tee sat there until he finished scoping out everything before he carry out his mission.

Tony called him to tell him that they needed to meet immediately. Tee stated, "Nigga, why is you burning my phone up, homie?"

Tony said, "Man, I have been trying to contact you for the last hour or so because I have some valuable information about that shit that happened down the street from my mother's house, cuz."

"Well, I'll get with you about that as soon as I'm through doing my thing, homie, so be patient, cuz. I have to get this shit right, and without a doubt I know you feel me on this 100 percent."

As Tee was sitting in his whip, he saw a car pull up about 12 feet behind him and seen someone get out and walk his way. Tee then heard a peck on his window and when he looked it was Tony.

"Tony, what the hell are you doing here, nigga?" Tee asked. "Man, you better start talking fast."

Tony got into the car and told Tee everything he found out about the case. Afterwards, Tee told Tony to get that gun from under his seat because he had just seen the nigga that wanted his head.

Jay pulled up at 10:30 p.m. on the dot, and he told Tee and Tony that he's about to go into the house and once he call, that's when they come in masked up with the units.

When they made it in the house about six rounds went off immediately, and that's when they all ran out the house then jumped into the whips and drove off.

When they made it to the expressway, Tee and Jay split up after the come to the exit at Mount Moriah and Hickory Hill. Tee went towards the south on Mount Moriah and Jay went west on Hickory Hill.

Tony was so paranoid and scared because he was already facing a case that he didn't do, and here he is accessory to felony murder with premeditation.

Tony told Tee that he want him to drop him off at his mom's house with the quickness.

Tee said, "Nigga, why are you so fuckin' shaky when we had masks on our faces?"

Tony replied, "I'm talking about this car we are in, Tee. Nigga, this car is stolen."

Tee replied, "That's why I'm on my way to ditch it around by the Wolf River and call Shay to come get us, cuz."

"Hell no!" Tony stated angrily. Then he said, "I'm pissed the fuck off, Tee. My life on the line as it is and nobody going to play with it."

So, when he heard that, Tee felt the anger in his voice, so he went ahead to drop him off at the bus stop and gave him $5 to get back to the Haven.

Tee drove off to ditch the car at a revolt area by the Wolf River until Shay get there while waiting at Germantown Parkway and Dexter.

While Tony was at the bus stop waiting on the 69 Shelby Drive and Hack Cross bus that goes through East Memphis he seen Jay passing by and flagged him down for a ride to the crib.

Tee made it to the corner of Macon and Sycamore View at the Shell gas station, and that's when he seen Shay pull up. Then he hopped in her 2008 Mustang Shelby GT 500.

Shay asked, "What the hell is going on with you, Tee?"

Tee replied to her instantly, "I need to get the hell out of here as soon as possible." Then he stated, "I just had to wreck shop on a nigga that was playing pistol games with me and my homies, sweetie."

"Baby, I need you to stay your ass out the streets because I don't want you to end up getting killed or placed in jail for some dumb shit."

Tee told Shay that he had no choice, but he will chill out on being in the streets.

Ring! Ring! Ring!

"Hello, one minute, please," Tee said to the other end of the phone.

"What you doing, baby?"

"Staying out the way," he said to Shay.

"Where the hell you at, anyway?" Shay replied.

Tee said, "I'm at the damn store."

"What you doing at the store when you shall be at the house, babe?"

Tee said, "I'm getting me something to eat, babe. Goddamn, a nigga can't even go to the fuckin' store. Baby, I'm not about to be in these streets like that, Shay. You don't have to act crazy like I need a fuckin' leash because I'm not a fuckin' dog."

She then said to Tee that she's pulling up at the store as she hung up the phone.

He walked out the store and seen Shay in her car looking mad as hell. Tee then walked up to the passenger side and opened the door.

"What?" She said, looking up at him as he got into the car. Then she said to him, "Are you going to tell me what the hell is going on with you, baby?"

Tee acted like he didn't hear a word she asked, and she folded her arms while looking out the window.

Shay told Tee, "Let's go home."

Tee said, "I'm waiting on Tony and Jay to arrive at the store."

Shay replied, "I didn't know you could talk."

Tee stated to her, "Shay, don't start this shit because it's a shit-load of shit going on right now. Baby, I need my car keys anyway, and I need them right fuckin' now, sweetie."

"Tee, I'm not giving you the keys, and you're not about to get back into the streets with your friends either."

"Look, Shay. Baby, I got something to do and I must take care of it immediately, baby."

"Okay, I'm gone give you these keys to your whip, but you better not get into any trouble or this time I'm done, babe."

Tee then said, "I'm gone come real and I just hope that you feel me on why I got to do what I got to do, sweetie. About a week ago Tony, Jay, and I went on a mission and made a stain that was worth $200,000, and that's how I was able to pay the bills and buy you that 2013 Mustang. Baby, I believe that someone is watching us, babe. I think they're watching our every move."

"What!" Shay replied. "Ya mean that someone is really watching us, Tee?"

"I don't know, but I'll let you know when I find out more about it, sweetie."

When Tee said that Tony and Jay pulled up at the store and Tony got out the car and then jumped into the car with Tee and Shay.

Tony said to drop them off in the Haven so he can get his things from Keisha's crib. So, Shay headed to the Haven to Keisha's apartments off Winchester.

Once Shay made it to the complex to drop off Tony, Tee told him that he'll catch up with him later. Afterwards, Tee and Shay went to the Graceland Inn on Elvis Presley Boulevard and got them a room for the night.

Tee walked to the customer service desk to place his order for a suite, and the receptionist gave him a key to room 103. Tee and Shay went to their room and when they walked in there, they begin to get comfortable. Then they went in the bathroom and hopped into the shower immediately.

When they got out the shower Shay told Tee that she gone rock his world as soon as the movie goes off.

Tee stated, "Baby, we don't have to wait on the movie to go off, we can start now if you really want these problems."

"Ha, ha, ha!" she laughed.

"What are you laughing for, baby?" Tee asked.

"I'm gone break your back tonight."

So Tee took his hands and slowly caress Shay's body passionately and then beginned foreplay. However, as soon as they started to have their sex flow the phone rung and it was Tony.

"What do you want, cuz? I'm trying to make love to my woman, and you want to interrupt me with some bullshit, I bet."

"Tee, it's really important. Just turn on the news and watch it for yourself, and then you'll see that I'm not on no bullshit."

Tee told Tony, "Thanks," and then turned on the news to see if they are talking about the robberies in East Memphis a few weeks ago. He knew that he had to stay on point because he's on the run for a lot of different shit, which is a robbery and double murder.

After seeing that shit on the news Tee knew that he could be going to jail if they catch up with him, and if that happens it will cause him to lose everything he has established in the past four years. Tee told himself to think of a master plan so that he can be prepared for the unexpected because he don't want to lose Shay in the process, mainly because of all the lies he'd told her and he wish that there was a way he could change the outcome of the whole situation and give a new approach to life itself.

Well, Tee felt like he might as well get him some just in case something happens to him in the wee of the night since they are at a hotel in the Haven, which is far away from their neighborhood. So, Tee started back kissing on her body from her feet to her lips as Shay felt the tender kisses from her man.

Then shay told him, "Remember these feelings from this sensation."

Shay and Tee begin doing the 69 on each other, and they both felt the pleasure and passion that ignited flames of love and affection, which were driven by the essence of exotic, profound, sexual healing followed by 100 percent love.

Tee undulated her hips to match him stroke for stroke as he tested her persistent love power intimately, which created multiple orgasms as she squirted from the bed to the wall. Shay's pussy was so damn wet that it flowed like a shimmering lake down her legs as well as his, and with every thrust in and out of Shay's pretty, shaven pussy while she moaned really hit Tee deep in his mind.

Tee knew that if he got caught the thought of losing what he has achieved would be useless and wouldn't be what he deserved.

CHAPTER 9

In today's news, there was a gang shootout in South Memphis. A man was shot several times. Police said they believe that the shooting had a lot to do with an East Memphis shooting two nights ago in which a man was shot in the neck. Not one arrest has been made or any tips been given to the police on that shooting."

It were the first thing Tee seen after he got through making love to Shay. Tee thought about Jay and Tony when he seen the clip on the shooting in South Memphis on TV news channel three.

"Hey, baby, how are you feeling today?" Shay asked.

Tee replied, "I'm fine right now, but I hope that nothing hasn't happen to Tony or Jay. I'm going to go to the south today to check on Tony and Jay since they're down the street from each other, sweetie."

Tee got out the bed and went into the bathroom to get himself together. After he finished he grabbed his car keys and ran out the hotel room to the valet parking and jumped in Shay's car.

Shay said, "Baby, I'm gone stay here until Keisha comes to pick me up for work."

"Okay," he stated.

"I'll be back at around 4:30 p.m. because we have to check out at 5 p.m., sweetheart."

"Alright then, sweetie."

Tee pulled out the parking lot and went to his destination. He got on the expressway at Elvis Presley and Brooks Road. Tee pushed it to the max, going 75 mph as he exited the e-way at the Lamar and Crump exit, and then pulled at Fourth and Vance to Jay's crib.

Tee got out the car and went to knock on the door, and as he was knocking, this dude came out of nowhere and shot Tee in the back and the neck.

Jay finally came to the door and see Tee layer there draped in blood. He screamed, "Oh, shit!"

Another homie came to the door and say, "Jay, hurry up and put him in the car, cuz, because we got to get him to the emergency room at Methodist Central Hospital."

Jay told the nurse that he needs help immediately, and they rushed Tee to the surgery room. Then Jay called Shay to let her know what happened to her man on his front porch of his home.

Shay answered the phone and she was like, "What is going on, Tee?"

Jay stated, "This not Tee, this Jay, and Tee just got shot in my front yard."

"Hell, no!" Shay replied. "He were coming to check on you and Tony because of what he seen on the news in your neighborhood, Jay."

Shay was so shocked to hear her man was shot, she told her supervisor that she had to leave for a family emergency. The supervisor asked what the emergency is, so Shay said, "My fiancé just got shot in South Memphis today and he's at the hospital in critical condition."

"Okay, then," her supervisor replied. I'll just get Stephanie to take up the day until this is done and you are 100 percent."

"Thanks! I'll surely work over when you need me to, Mrs. Coleman."

The nurse came out the emergency room and told Jay that he's gone make it and he will be able to walk still. "The bullet missed his spinal cord by three inches, and his artery by one inch, so he's good, and in about six to 12 months he shall be fully recovered."

Shay finally arrived at the Methodist Central Hospital and seen Jay. When she seen him she asked him, "Where is Tee housed at?"

Jay replied, "He's in room 103. They have gotten the bullets taken out of his neck and back. He is all wrapped up in bandages and barely can talk."

"Hey, babe, are you alright?" Shay asked. "I hope that you are feeling better because it scared me to hear that this happened to you, babe." Then she said, "I love you with all my heart, body, and soul, sweetie."

Tee said in a slurred voice, "I love you too. I can't wait 'til this bed rest is over because I will get my revenge." After he stated that he said "That shit hurts. After my last mission I'm leaving the streets to live a quiet life of love, peace, and happiness."

The phone started ringing and Shay answered the phone. "Hello, who is this?"

"It's Tony and Keisha. Is Tee okay?"

"Yes, he's doing better," Shay told Tony and Keisha.

Tony and Keisha told Shay that they are on the way there and,

"It's sad to hear that happened to Tee today, but in the street life, that type of shit happen every day and anybody can be a victim in this crooked-ass world called Babylon."

Tony and Keisha made it there to be with their friends, and Tony told Shay that whenever he find out who did this, revenge is a must.

As Tee laid there in the hospital bed on life support from being shot Tony started shedding tears along with Jay too. All of a sudden, Tee failed into an induced coma and his eyes rolled back in his head, then the nurses ran in and placed him on the machine to monitor his heart rate.

They waited to see if there will be any other movement from this situation, and Shay begin to get down on her knees to pray for him.

She prayed that God will let him make it through despite all of the things that he and his homeboys have done in this lifetime. While she were praying, Tony, Keisha, and Jay followed suit. After they got through praying the doctor told them that visitation hours are now over. So, they all kiss Tee on the cheek and left the hospital as they went their separate ways.

Jay and Tony went searching for information on the shooting of Tee in the community. They wanted to know who did this to Tee, and when they find out, it's on.

A year had passed, and Tony found out that a rival gang is the reason Tee ended up getting shot, and since Tee is sitting in his hospital bed on life support from that shooting, Tony called Jay to let him know that a rival gang shot Tee.

Tony asked Jay, "Will you help me get revenge for Tee?"

Jay said, "Give me a couple hours to get some guns and ammo because I know the car when I see it. Tony, these are the same niggas that we took that safe from, cuz."

Tony asked, "What house?"

"That house over on Hernando and Linden by the FedEx Forum while you were in jail on that shit about the store, cuz. They use the same car in the shooting of another rival gang in South Memphis two weeks ago, as well as the shooting in East Memphis at the Citgo gas station. They have been on some real banging shit lately, and that is about to end now as we speak, cuz. We have to avenge Tee with honor and integrity."

While this was being put into play Shay went back to the hospital to sit with Tee and prayed so hard that Tee tried to reach out with his hand to touch Shay. She begin to smile, and said to Tee, "I thought I lost you, baby." But he still couldn't talk from the bullet wound to his neck.

While she was holding his hand her phone rang constantly until she decided to answer it. It was Jay. He asked her, "How is Tee pulling through?"

She replied, "He's coming along, but still isn't speaking."

"Alright. If you need anything, call me and I will do it for you until my homie get well and comprehensive enough to function."

Shay told Jay, "Thanks, I love you like a brother," and then the phone call ended.

Shay had tears still running down her eyes from the hurt she's encountered from this tragedy, but she were determined to be there for her man regardless of what is happening at work.

Tony and Keisha was sitting at the house watching channel 3 news and seen the same car Jay said somebody used in a drive-by a few weeks ago. Keisha said she believe that they were the niggas from around the way of Cottonwood and Perkins and probably who shot Tee in the back and neck.

Tony said, "How do you know that, Keisha?"

She replied, "I recognize the faces they're showing on the news, baby."

"Hmmm, baby, you might be right, and if you are, things will be better for my homie once he get better. I know that there are so much going on, and when you're lying low most of the time you hear the streets talking. Soon I'll find out who actually tried to kill my homeboy, and thanks to the streets, news, and the police word of mouth traveling gratefully, I do know that it'll all play in our favor or it could lead us down a road of destruction, as well."

Tony stated that so truthfully. He also stated, "You have to forgive to be forgiven, but never forget because in this world you'll see that you're faced with the unexpected."

Back at the hospital where Shay is sitting with her man, she told Tee that she's glad he's pulling through and regaining the strength he needs to speak.

Once she heard him say "I love you" several times in a 30-minute span, his heart rate begin to rise to normal fast as it could and his body begin to function properly minute by minute. Shay was very excited and lost for words, so she just kissed him gratefully on his lips as tears flowed joyfully.

When Tee felt her kiss, he rose up and spoke clearly saying, "Shay, I love you to death and I want to marry you when I get out of this hospital."

Her phone started to ring and it was Stephanie asking how Tee's doing. Shay replied, "Fantastic! Girl, I heard the feds had you helmed up around the time this happened to my man."

Stephanie said, "That Jay entourage was slipping in the trap house when I were over there," Shay said. "Girl, I know that isn't what happened when Tee got shot!" Stephanie told Shay that Jay said he came to the door after he heard gunshots and found Tee bleeding on his porch from the gunshots fired at Tee.

"Where did you get your information from, girl?"

Stephanie replied, "I was there selling that ooh-wee, if you know what I mean, girl."

Shay said, "Girl, I know what you talking about. You ain't got to be so bashful about whoring because money is money and you need it survive, girl. Anyway, have you seen Tony and Keisha today?"

Stephanie said, "I haven't seen Tony since I last fucked him and sucked his dick. So, he's with that bitch Keisha who thinks she's better than me, huh? She's the neighborhood freak and I'm considered a whore because I get paid for sex and she don't."

Shay said, "Girl, you too beautiful and you don't have to deal with haters by being jealous right along with them because she's fuckin' Tony like you were in the past."

Stephanie told Shay, "Thanks, you're totally right because she's doing her and I'm doing me."

Then Shay told Stephanie, "Be careful and cautious while you're in those streets, girl."

She replied, "Thanks, Shay! Tell Tee much love and get well soon." Then the call ended.

Shay sat back thinking to herself saying when Tee leave the hospital what he's actually gone do about getting revenge after he said he wanted to marry her? She really was happy to hear it coming from him after all that they have been through over the years. She thought about the time that Lanetta told her how good Tee was to her and how they were soulmates. And then she thought about how happy Lanetta were with him every day.

Shay always mimic that type of relationship with a real man, and she got the opportunity once Lanetta ended up getting killed. But little did she know, Lanetta were always cheating with Corey behind Tee's back. If Shay knew Tee was the one who killed Corey and Lanetta, then she probably wouldn't be with Tee or feel how she feel about Tee because Lanetta were her best friend from childhood.

Out of all the thoughts in her head about the type of relationship she wants, Tee rose up and hugged her and told her that he is feeling better than he ever felt before he got shot. Then he explained to her his life in the streets is definitely over after he gets revenge.

Shay told him, "Don't seek revenge because you might not come out on top and end up six feet under."

Tee replied, "I'm gone get them niggas who shot me if I ever see them again.

Then the phone rang and Shay answered it, "Hello?" It was Tony and he told Shay when Tee get 100 percent he know who tried to take Tee out. Shay told him to please keep it to himself because she don't want to lose Tee again because he told her is going to get his revenge after he's released from the hospital.

Tony told Shay that he understood her and as his big sister he would keep it to himself, but something has to be done to those niggas as quickly as possible. "Jay and I gone take care of it for Tee, so you don't have to worry about nothing at all, Shay. I love you, Shay, and Tee is like my own family. So, when someone mess with my family, they mess with me, sis," Tony stated.

Shay replied, "Thanks Tony for handling this for him. If Tee needs to give you anything afterwards, just let me know because you deserve to be compensated for putting that work in, cuz."

CHAPTER 10

It's early in the morning and Shay decided to go see her man at the hospital and take him breakfast. Tee was awakened by the smell of some homemade waffles, sausages, eggs, and buttermilk biscuits Shay had cooked.

He told his soon-to-be wife that it's a blessing to be alive and that he's very appreciative of her being there for him when he needed her the most.

The nurse walked into his room and told him that he'll be going home today, and then she said to Tee, "Make sure that you go to therapy twice a week for your neck. This is so you can get use to turning it again from left to right and right to left."

After the nurse explained to Tee his therapy, a big, fat smile came across his face, and Shay was happy now that she could feel like a woman again affectionately.

Shay haven't had any dick for a year, two months, and three days, and her pussy was hungry like two fat bitches stuffing their mouths with steaks 14 pounds thick, that's how bad Shay wanted some dick. Shay begin to take his dick into her warm, fierce mouth and wrap her lips around the head of Tee's dick. She took her tongue swirling it around his shaft while slurping his dick passionately after she felt the hardness in her throat.

Tee lifted her chin up as he took her by the head with his hands and then fuck her mouth until she couldn't take no more. After Tee reached his peak he exploded in her mouth as she swallowed every drop of his cum, then Shay moaned in ecstasy. Tee took his dick and entered her juicy pussy with every inch of him and undulated her hips to match his every move as he climbed deeper and deeper inside Shay's juicy pussy 'til he climaxed.

Then Shay had multiple orgasms one more time which was from the essence of erotic pleasure driven by romance wholeheartedly.

They never knew what hit them from the lovemaking they encountered, but after they were finished, the phone rang and it was Tony on the line. He's one of Tee's soldiers.

Tony were ready to go put in this work for Tee on the niggas who shot him. "What's up, Tee?" Tony asked.

"Nothing, homie, but about to get ready to get groomed for the day."

"Well, let's meet at 7:30 p.m., cuz," Tony said.

Tee stated, "Okay."

Tony said, "I'm working hard to get them niggas, cuz. Oh yeah, Jay said if you need anything holler at him ASAP."

"Well, Shay just called me to the room and I'll hit you up when I'm on my way, cuz, so stay safe, homeboy. That's what's up," Tony said as he hung up the phone.

Tee asked, "What ya want, Shay?"

"Tee, please come back to bed and stay here with me, sweetie."

"Babe, I got to check a few traps and I'll be back soon. Tony and I have some niggas to get together."

Shay stated, "Jay will bring you some things to help you through the day while I make these Ben Franklins, honey."

The phone rang again and this time it was Keisha, who said, "What's up, girl?"

Shay replied, "Shit here but chilling by myself, girl."

Keisha said, "Do you want to go out shopping or will you like to go to the movies, girl?"

Shay said, "It's cool. What time you gone be ready?"

"I'll be ready in about an hour or so and I'll call you when I'm done getting ready, girl."

Now that Tee and Tony is on a manhunt for the niggas that shot him, it's really getting to his head because retaliation is a must in his mind. But all Tee could visualize was Shay saying "stay here with me, baby." Tee constantly blocked out what his wife told him because of his determination for revenge, so while he looked for them, Tee was in pain.

The phone rang for three minutes until Keisha finally answered it and Shay said, "Come on, girl. I'm outside your house." So, Keisha came running out and jumped into the car with Shay.

Shay pulled off and they spotted Tee's car at the Shell gas station. Shay dialed his number, and the phone rang twice before Tee answered.

"Hello!" Tee replied.

Shay asked, "Tee, where are you and Tony going?"

Tee replied to her, "We are going to meet up with Jay to discuss some business."

Then Shay said, "Baby, be careful and make sure you call me later because me and Keisha are going to the movies to see

'Kingdom Come.'"

Tee told her he love her and hung up. "Now it's time to get down to business, Tony," Tee stated. They pulled up to Jay's crib and Jay jumped in the truck with several units and plenty ammo.

They all were strapped up in all areas and dressed in Army fatigues like Navy Seals as they headed to East Memphis. Tee put in that Tupac Shakur CD and played his favorite song "Hit 'Em Up" and was ready to ambush them niggas that shot him in the back and neck in South Memphis.

They came way out of pocket to try to kill Tee and put him in a coma for a year, but now it's their turn to feel the rise of a menace.

While Tee and his homies are on a mission to kill Shay and Keisha was out having a good time together, and Stephanie called Shay.

Shay never answered, so she called Tee's phone, and Tee answered and said, "Who is this?"

"This Stephanie!" she said to Tee. "I see the niggas that shot you that day over here on Winchester and Goodlett at the Mapco."

Tee said, "Thanks!" and hit the slab so that he can pull up on them before they leave this gas station. So, Tee hit 385 East and jumped off on the Winchester exit.

Tony rolled down his window and cocked his 45 Desert Eagle so he could bust at the driver as he attempted to get back into his car.

Tee pulled closer to the entrance and unloaded 150 rounds until he blew up their car and sped off into the night. His job was finished, and his life has just begun as well as his future with Shay.

Most of all, Shay and Keisha was still at the movies watching "Kingdom Come" and they met two brothers who offered them dinner at a restaurant. Shay said she couldn't accept dinner from any men that isn't hers.

Keisha told Shay that, "Tee won't know unless you tell him, so what's crackin, Shay?"

"Girl, you know that I'm a faithful woman to whoever I'm with, Keisha, so stop trying to make me out to be as fake as other women are to their spouse. I have integrity and honor for the man I love in spite of how he run the streets all the time. Besides, I love Tee as much as Lanetta did when she were alive despite all the drama that was going on with them. Anyway, Keisha."

"Well, girl, I'm gone leave with them and I'll get back with you later, Shay," Keisha replied.

"Okay. I will see you later, and please be careful dealing with him and his brother because I don't want nothing to happen to you at all, girl. You are truly the only friend I have since my best friend got murdered. I don't want to lose another friend to these wicked streets because I have lost one already and almost lost my man, as well. I just don't see the point to cheat when you already know the outcome of it and its consequences. Keisha, please stay safe and start taking care of yourself better than you are because all sex ain't good sex, if you get what I'm telling you, girl."

"Shay, I know that. I don't fuck everyone I meet on the first day we are kicking it, so just believe in me when I tell you that as a friend, Shay. We have been knowing each other since high school and college, and you have never heard about me sleeping with any and every one I meet."

"As an exception, I know that came about by that bitch Stephanie because she hates the ground I walk on, Shay."

"I know that Keisha, and I apologize for just looking out for your wellbeing, girl. I'll stop being paranoid about a lot of things, girl," Shay stated.

"I understand, Shay, and I really appreciate your concern for my life, Shay, because that what friends are for at the end of the day," Keisha said.

"I'm about to get back to the house before Tee comes home from Jay's house," Shay told Keisha.

"Alright, girl, I'll talk to you later." Keisha hugged Shay and left with the brothers.

As soon as Keisha left, Shay hit speed dial on her cellphone and called Tee to see what he was doing at the moment.

Tee answered the phone and said, "Baby, what you want now?"

Shay replied, "I need you to make your way to the house."

Tee replied, "I'll be on my way as soon as we get through doing this job, sweetie."

Afterwards, Shay said in a deep, sassy voice, "don't be out all night either."

Tee replied, "I'm not gone be too much longer. What in the world is wrong with you, babe? I noticed that ever since I got out of the hospital you have been riding a nigga like a fuckin' stalker. Baby, stop that shit, sweetie! Baby, I want you to know that I love you and will always love you, so stop acting like one of these flings in the streets. There are a whole lot of things that we could be achieving if you will just be cool. Let me continue to do me, babe, because I just want you to know that as long as I'm legit there's no reason to worry, Shay."

"Okay, baby. I promise to stop treating you like some fuckin' dog on a leash, and I will trust that you will stay out of trouble, as well."

"Thanks, babe."

"See you later, sexy sunshine," Tee said to her. Now that he promised to stay out of harm's way if she just would chill out she won't have to be worried. Tee was so serious about he said to her from the bottom part of his heart. Tee knew that Shay was not gone buy it, but he had to let her know he is a man of his word.

As she could see it, Tee never wanted to hurt her no matter

what the situation was or may have been with her. But it was Tee who stated, "Shay, I hope that you are aware of the way that you are trying to treat me, sweetie, because you must think I'm a damn fool." Tee ended that conversation with that and walked out the door.

CHAPTER 11

It's been two years since Tee got his revenge, and his life is starting to unfold with Tony's death, which took place 18 months later in North Memphis at the Corned Beef House. Now that his right-hand man gone Tee starts depending on Shay for all his business in the streets, until one day Tee was arrested for five counts of first-degree premeditated murder, which was from two years ago. While he was at the mall shopping, the police caught up with him.

Now all his business will have to be done by Shay now, and while he is in jail Shay made sure her man was straight by making sure his lawyers got paid.

Shay helped him get out of jail at trial by testifying for her man with all honesty, and she told the jury that he was with her when the store owner got killed and robbed. He was with her when that shooting in East Memphis took place at the Maple-wood Apartments, and he was with her when the shooting took place in South Memphis on Imogene and Silver Street. Then Shay told them when he went to his homeboy's house in South Memphis he was shot in the neck and back with a 45 caliber that almost took his life.

"He was in a coma for approximately one year." She said, "On August 19, 1999 Tee went to my mom's house and helped her with mowing her mom's yard, and on October 3, 1999 he went to this party with me and we was at the party until at least 11:20 p.m. Then we went back to the house and took it in for the night together."

The judge said in a brief statement, "Well, I'm gone go into recess until tomorrow, and then we will start this trial back at 10 a.m. in perfect settings. You all can leave and don't discuss any details about this case with anyone or anybody."

Shay looked at Tee and left the courtroom to go make his bond since the judge allowed Tee to get a bond, and as she walked over to Memphis Bonding Company to holler at CJ, she paid $25,587 on that bond for Tee.

Around about 7:30 p.m. Shay was waiting for her man to walk out them doors, and when he walked out of them jail doors, Shay ran and jumped on him with her legs wrapped all around him. She begin kissing and squeezing him tight around his neck where he got shot at because she were so excited to have him back with her until it's time to go back to court on those murders.

Shay's heart begin melting because she had to do some things that she didn't want to do, but it was for her man, so she got about it.

She heard the phone ring and answered it, saying "Hello!"

It was Jay asking her, "How did this happened to Tee when he stated he was changing his ways, Shay?"

Shay replied, "He still was dealing with Tony's death and word on the streets was you, Tony, and my man killed those five dudes at the Mapco in East Memphis."

Jay asked, "Where that come from, Shay? Who spread that type of rumor?"

Shay said she didn't know, but she's getting Tee out of jail by any means necessary.

Jay told her, "I'll give you $100,000 at 5 p.m. after I make a few sales."

Shay told him she's straight and that she'll get it herself. Because of her alter ego she didn't trust Jay and never has trusted him since he came home from the feds, especially when the police ran up in Stephanie's house and busted her and Tony.

Now that it's 10 a.m. Shay and Tee just pulled up at the Shelby County Criminal Justice Center and had to find them a parking spot before they headed to the courthouse with Tee's attorney Scott Hall.

As the hearing started Shay and Tee sat in their chairs waiting on Judge Benet to enter the courtroom, and as soon as the Bailiff walked in he said, "All rise, the Honorable Judge Fredrick Benet is residing. You may be seated."

"Ladies and gentlemen of the court, I, Judge Fredrick Benet, bring these charges of premeditated first degree murder on the defendant by a sworn impaneled jury on this day of October 3, 1999. As part of the proceedings, I make this ruling as the 13th juror to find the defendant not guilty based on the prosecution obtaining illegal evidence through bribery, so the case is dismissed with prejudice."

Tee and his wife Shay was in all smiles after the verdict for murder in the first degree. After they got out the courtroom Tee seen Keisha and Jay walking up the stairs and he yelled their names out loud, "Keisha, Jay, over here, cuz. I just got all the charges dismiss with prejudice and I'm free from the system."

"What a blessing, homie."

"I am ready to get out of these streets and walk a straight line for the rest of my life. I already lost my childhood friend Tony, and that's why it's time to retire before I lose mine. Life is too short to constantly play with it like we do in those streets, Jay. I know that you might don't care at all, and always remember that karma is going to always prevail no matter what. I'm gone start going to Rastafarian Groundings in North Memphis on Broad Street. I know that I will learn how to deal with the trickery of Babylon and its government once and for all. If you love me like you say you do, homie, you will respect my decision and follow along to righteousness and consciousness, cuz. We are family and we are always doing negative shit but never no positive shit, so what's up? Are you down to trod Rasta or what?"

Jay said, "Cuz, I'm down for whatever, and that is the coolest thing that you have ever said to me, nigga. I know a little about the Rasta movement and it's wonderful once you get deep into it."

Tee then replied, "That's what's up, cuz! I will be going to it tomorrow because I'm gone take it as I took the streets, Jay."

"What have you been doing since you have been back on the streets with your girl? Have you even asked her to marry you yet? I heard you say that you are ready in the hospital, or was that just talk? Tee, are you going to do it for real? I think that you should, cuz, and the reason is that she held you down 103 percent when you were arrested on August 19, 1999. Shay is a good woman, and I want to see my homie happy for a change. I know that Tony's death was a hurtful thing, but there's nothing that we can do to bring him back, so it's time that we get on our grown man shit."

Tee smiled at Jay as he said in a sarcastic tone, "Where you learn that at, cuz?"

Jay replied, "Homie, you act like I'm just dumb 'cause I run the streets a lot selling that weight. I'm very educated and intelligence is my persona 103 percent, cuz. Well, it's getting late, homie, and it's time to get back to the crib. Tee, tell Shay I said hello and I miss her so much, cuz. Also, let her know I said that you all shall gone get married as soon as possible."

"Okay," Tee replied, "as soon as I get home in about a couple of hours."

Jay then jumped into his car and left. Then Tee jumped in his whip to leave Jay's spot and he saw Mike and Keisha heading to the store at the corner of Winchester.

He yelled, "What's up, cuz? Where are you two going?"

Mike said, "Going to buy some drinks and some blunts to take with us over Keisha's house."

Tee replied with a smile, "You about to get your freak on, huh?"

Mike said with another smile, "Hell, yeah!"

Tee drove off to the house to get to his soon-to-be wife Shayla Smith.

CHAPTER 12

It's Saturday morning and Tee just woke up and washed his face and brushed his teeth while waiting for Shay to get up.

Tee came out the bathroom as he headed to the kitchen to fix him some breakfast, and since he were in the kitchen, Shay walked in as she asked him what he's cooking.

Tee said, "Babe, I'm making you breakfast in bed, but since you up already, I'll just bring it to the table."

Shay then asked, "Why are you cooking me breakfast? What's the occasion on this new thing, sweetheart?"

Tee replied, "I just want to show you that I am that type of man, as well. Baby, you deserve all the things I'm able to give you on a daily basis. I want you to be treated like you deserve to be treated, my queen, because I hope that isn't a problem, sweetie."

"Oh, no. Actually, I really appreciate it wholeheartedly, Tee.

So, how long this gone last, though?"

"Baby, I'm gone be that king that I said I were gone be to you from the get go. When you first encountered me after Lanetta's death, I told you that I was that man for you, Shay."

Shay replied, "I would like to know the truth on a few things, though."

"What's that, Shay?" Tee said.

She stated, "I would like to know if you really meant what you said to me on your deathbed."

Tee replied, "Yes, baby, I meant every bit of the words I spoke to you in the hospital. The question is, when are you ready to plan our wedding?"

Shay said, "As soon as possible, my king!"

"Well, you need to get on the ball because I have some ring shopping to do today."

While Shay was getting ready to freshen up, she ate breakfast first, and then Tee told her he's on his way to look for that special ring.

So, he jumped into his car and his phone rung. "Who is this calling me?" he stated, then he answered it, and it was Shay.

"What's the problem, sweetie? I told you that I'm going to look for our wedding rings."

Shay said, "I just wanted to say I love you."

"Okay, sweetheart, I love you too."

Tee hung up as he begin to drive off into the sunset, then he put his favorite CD in the CD player and turned the volume up on 6kws. He was bumping Tupac's "Two of America's Most Wanted" while he was heading to the jewelry store. He stopped at the red light then pull out a cigarette to fire it up when the police stopped right beside him.

Then the police noticed that Tee was wanted for robbery and pulled him over on the spot. The police told him that he have to go see the detectives for questioning downtown. Tee was like, "For what?"

They said to him, "We have a warrant for your arrest on aggravated robbery that happened on November 3, 2001, which was at the Shell gas station in South Memphis off Bellevue and Parkway."

His whole mind went blank because he didn't know what else to say or do at that point 'cause he knew they were full of shit. Tee knew that they were trying to just get him for something because they were mad he beat them out at trial to get his freedom back. So, they're trying to pin an aggravated robbery on him, so he called Shay and told her to get a lawyer to make his bond because he's been arrested again.

When Tee made it to 201 Poplar Avenue they sent him to the 11th floor to speak with Detective Alan Smith, who is the head robbery detective. He asked Tee, "Where was you on November 3, 2001?"

Tee replied, "I was at the house with my wife."

"What was you and your wife doing at the time of the robbery?"

Tee stated to him, "I'm gone let her tell you when she get here."

"Okay, smartass!" the detective replied. "I see that you want to be hard. Well, I have something for people like you."

So, Detective Alan Smith sent Tee to jail and told him that when he want to talk, give him a call.

When Tee got to lower level to be processed in he seen another one of his childhood friends, and then told Mane that Tony got gunned down as soon as he got out of jail for those robberies and murders.

Mane said, "Tee, I hate that happened, and I hope that his mom and sisters are okay. I hope that you are coming along since that tragedy, homie."

Tee said to Mane, "Cuz, I know that he's in a better place now, but it still gets to me at times."

"Why are you here now, Tee?"

"Well, they said that I had a warrant for aggravated robbery. I know I haven't robbed anyone, but they insist on thinking that it was me who robbed that gas station in South Memphis."

"Well, I hope they find out who did it, and when they do, I hope he own up to his charge or at least help you out, cuz."

"Mane, I know Shay is gone go berserk on me. Cuz, I hate that I have to take her through this again."

"Homie, you just got to tell her that you haven't did anything and they harassed you while you were at the mall shopping for the ring."

Tee told him that he had just beat them out on all those charges they tried to stick him with a month ago. Then Tee stated, "I just don't know what's up with this system anymore."

It's 8 a.m. and the cells finally opened for dayroom rec. Tee is able to call Shay now so he could let her know why he couldn't answer his phone no more yesterday. Tee walked to the phone in the day room, and he picked up the receiver to dial Shay number, so when it ringed the first time it just kept ringing until Shay picked up.

The phone stated, "You have a collect call from the Shelby County Jail from Tee. To accept press one, to decline press zero." Shay accept the call and asked Tee, "What the hell did you do? You were supposed to be shopping for our wedding bands!"

"Baby, I was at the red light when the police pulled up and said to me that they got a warrant for my arrest for an aggravated robbery. I was like, that isn't me you all are looking for, but they said I have to go talk to the detectives downtown. Baby, I really wasn't doing anything this time. I hope that you have enough money to get me a lawyer or we can use Scott Hall again since he's the family lawyer."

"Okay, baby, I will get him to handle this. But when it's over, I'm sure in the hell hope that you didn't really have nothing to do with the charge."

"I love you, Shay, with all my heart and soul. I will always love you as long as breath is in my body."

Shay said, "I love you too, Tee, but we have to get over these humps that is constantly causing us to be distanced."

"Baby, what a man supposed to do when the stakes is against him? Being a black man, I know that the system is crooked as hell when it comes to the black race."

Shay said to him, "It's your job to be able to stay out of trouble, Tee."

"Baby, you're absolutely right."

"In the meantime, just keep your head up in there until I'm able to get the money for the bail bondsmen, baby. We will beat this from the streets, my king."

"Okay, Shay," Tee replied.

"Well, it's one minute 'til this p hone hang up, and I'll call you when you get off of work later, my sexy, caramel, vanilla sensation."

At 10 p.m. Jay pulled up at the Shelby County Jail to go put money on Tee's books so he can get the items he need on commissary, which is truly his way of keeping him from getting flap by the laws. Once he did that he left immediately so he wouldn't get questioned by the deputy jailers at the account window. He made his way outside to his truck and pulled off in the heat of the night.

Jay's heart start pumping fast as sweat begin to run across his forehead why it was raining. When he got on the Expressway he called Shay, but she didn't answer. She was kicking it with this dude name Carl Smith, which were her best friend, and she was telling him what she been going through.

It was about 1 a.m. and Shay tells Carl to stay at the house with her to keep her safe until the morning, then she'll drop him off on her way to work.

Carl told her to never worry about her problems because God will make a way for Tee to get out.

Shay replied, "Thanks Carl for the good advice, and that's why I love talking to you when I need to talk the most."

It was Sunday morning and Tee just woke up from a good dream of him and Shay. He got out the bed to wash his face and brush his teeth as he waited for the cells to roll open so he could call his wife Shay.

While he waits patiently for rec in the day room, he was told by another cellmate his wife is cheating on him with a sucka. Tee ignored the comment because he knew that his wife wouldn't never cheat on him.

The cells finally rolled for rec and Tee went straight to the phone and dial Shay's cellphone as the phone rang, it rang and rang until Shay picked up the phone.

"Hello," she said in a tired, slurred voice.

Tee replied, "Hello, baby. What's been going on since we last talked? What is up with my lawyer?"

She said, "They're investigating your case and they said that you shall be out in a few months. Baby, I got something to tell you and I hope that you appreciate it because I don't want you to be mad. I've been hanging with Carl and Keisha and we're trying to get the money to make your bond next week. It's been so hard, but I got your back, baby. You hear me, Tee?"

Afterwards, Tee told Shay to get the money from Jay and Shay said, "Jay isn't fit to be fucked with because he's still working for the feds. Baby, that's why I'm dealing with Carl and Keisha because Jay is a snake, baby."

"Anyway, I've given my life to Jah since I've been in here and it's been great spending time with my creator, Jah Rastafari. Baby, Jah has taught me the truth about I-n-I in inity (unity), love, peace, and black manhood. Well baby, if you believe Jay is a snake, then don't worry about getting anything from him because Jah Rastafari will provide I——n-I with finances to get I-n-I out."

Shay told Tee that she'll be by his side and the phone hung up.

As the days go by, Tee is learning more about who he is as a black man through Rastafari. It's been a week since he talked to Shay or anyone. Now that Tee is finding out he gone have to do some time for murder on count one he's considering taking 10 years on that because he don't want to end up with life. Since he beat them out on four counts of murder in the first degree he figured it's the best option for him and his family to leave the state of Tennessee when he gets out this time.

This was the best thing that he ever said to Shay, and she agreed with him because she were ready to leave anyway.

Tee told her it'll probably be in a few months before they can leave Tennessee because he's still on parole.

So, Shay replied, "Baby, we can wait until then if you want to, but I have to apply for another job, Tee. So, we'll wait until we both are straight."

CHAPTER 13

It's Monday morning and it's 8 a.m. the cell doors just rolled opened, so Tee ran out into the day room. While in the day room Tee try to call Shay and still didn't get no answer. Shay haven't been answering her phone or been to visit him lately. Tee really is messed up in the head because Shay is his first and only love. He's been with her since college, and the thought of her not being there anymore makes him mad at the world. However, this time the phone said, "That number is restricted," and Tee was mad as hell because he's given her the world and more.

Knowing that he's lost everything he ever owned since going to jail, he called Jay, and when Jay answered the phone and said, "What's up, cuz?"

Tee asked, "Have you seen Shay lately?"

Jay replied, "She's been with that bitch Keisha and some nigga name Carl since you been locked up, cuz. I think that she and Keisha and that nigga Carl are doing things together 'cause they are always kicking it, cuz."

"Anyway, Jay, I need ya help while I do this 10-year bit because when I come home it is gone be a gangsta party like never before, cuz."

"I'll see ya, homeboy! What you need right now, cuz?"

"Just send me $300 to my account and I'll take it from there, cuz."

Jay replied, "Alright, homie," and hung up.

Tee got off of the phone and went back to the cell until lunch time. Then he begin to reminisce about everything he's done. While thinking about all the people he helped and the only one kept it real was Jay. The one Shay claim that was a snake is the one that came through for me when she was the biggest snake of them all, which inclined his mind to trust no woman with his heart ever again.

Tee became someone that he never thought he would become from the life he lived in the game, but his last thoughts was to do this little time like a gangsta. He thought when he get out of jail he's gone be with that grind hard mentality as well as be harder than ever on a bitch and a whore like nothing exist, which is what he did after he made up his mind.

Tee said that he want to start with professional women since his relationship with Shay turned out to be fake. Even though Shay left him hanging, he only became stronger mentally, physically, and spiritually. As time passed, Tee wanted to start off good when he get out of prison. Tee's alter ego didn't want to let go of the streets, but he said he's gone trod the livity of Rastafari.

Now that it's 8:30 p.m. and they holler lockdown, Tee went in his cell and mark his calendar, knowing he's about to flatten a 10-year sentence for first degree murder.

As the nightfall passes by and daylight entered Tee and P-Bands' cell, they arose to the occasion as they got prepared for breakfast. Morning breakfast was sausage, eggs, and biscuits with orange juice and some grape jelly. It wasn't the typical meal Tee and P-Bands wanted, but it held them over.

While Tee was eating, P-Bands went to get on the phone to call his wife, China Doll, who worked at the shake joint on Getwell and Winchester. She was the queen of the shaker and she told P-Bands that her friend wanted somebody to talk to and get to know. So, P-Bands told her that he would relate the message to his cellmate, and by the time Tee came out the cell and P-Bands said, "My wife's friend want to get at ya, cuz," and then he gave Tee the phone.

Once they started talking to each other, Tee asked her what was her name. She replied, "Caramel Mocha," and that's when Tee told her, "I'm all about them dividends and nothing else."

Then she said, "That's what I'm all about as well. I want us to build a team when you touch down, Tee."

"Okay," Tee replied, "that's the type of woman I need on my team."

Afterwards the phone hung up and P-Bands told Tee that he get out on October 12, 2006, and when he leave he's gone stay in touch with him. Tee told him to stay out there, as well as stay sucka-free until he touch down on the town.

P-Bands gave Tee all his info to get in touch with him, and when the time came for P-Bands to walk out them prison walls, Tee threw him $2,000 he made off selling them boxins and heroin packs. P-Bands said, "Thanks, cuz! I'll get up with Jay and keep you straight until you touch the streets in 2008, cuz."

Tee started working on getting in college for business administration, but he could only get online courses in prison, and when he took up those courses and learned how to go into business legit, he wrote out a plan for a club called Cosmos and he got it copyrighted as soon as possible.

Jay came to visit Tee at the prison in the afternoon and told him that he could use his house as a house plan for parole and his lawn business for his job plan. Tee was so happy to see Jay, which he asked him, "What is Shay doing out there in those streets?"

Jay said, "Her and that nigga Carl have been really close lately, and her and Keisha be going over there all the time now, cuz."

Tee stated, "So, the whore want to have me in here all by myself and insane, huh? Well, I guess that I'll write her a letter today and let her know that she ain't messing with no desperate-ass man."

Jay said, "Cuz, the hell with Shay! You need to start thinking about what you gone do when you do get back on the streets."

So, Tee stated in an angry voice, "I'm gone show her who's the boss and who's the trick. Then she will know that she had the best man ever."

"Cuz, it's time to go now, but I will come see you in about a couple of weeks because I got to go to the Plug to pick up 30 keys of that good cocaine, if you know what I mean, homie."

Tee said with a smile on his face, "I know exactly what you mean, cuz. I hope that you see straight on your trip. Watch out for the laws and be very attentive of the highways, and make sure you keep some sardines in the cut for the scent."

"Okay, homie," Jay replied. "I'll get at you later."

After Jay left Tee went back to his cell block and he seen another friend that used to be like his brother to the fullest. He knew that he was about to go up for parole, but instead he just commence to stabbing him in his neck and kidneys because of what he remembered. Tee just freaked out completely.

With that nigga's blood all over his hands and clothes, Tee realized how traumatic he had gotten over the years. The root of this massacre caused him to start losing all the true people he loved dearly. Tee just wasn't himself anymore, and he couldn't even believe that he did something like that two weeks before his parole date. But with all those thoughts running through his head he just felt betrayed deeply inside his soul.

Tee went to the hole for 30 days and was evaluated for mental illness, and the doctor discovered that Tee suffered from post-traumatic stress disorder, schizophrenia, and major depression. The doctor prescribed him to take Loxapine and Celexa, and when Tee realized he just fucked his parole date off he knew that he have to do another year before he flatten his sentence if they do not charge with assault and battery.

Tee went to the mental health program so that he could stay out the way of violence and abusing those people that mess with him because he was truly ready to get out of prison. It is so crazy that a man of his character had to endure so many turmoils and hills to be able to see clearly of what's life all about. The fact that it took prison to receive this logical thinking truly have made Tee a better man mentally, morally, and spiritually.

While in the cell meditating and talking to Jah for guidance and for a path towards love and peace, he was told by the Correctional Officer that he had a visit. It was a big surprise when he walked into visitation because it was Shay and he couldn't even believe his eyes.

After all that he thought of her from these last few years of doing this time, he wondered why this tramp come to see him now? But as he went to be seated, she told him that she really miss him and would like a hug.

Tee said angrily, "Why shall I give your ass a hug when you have been out there kissing and fucking every other nigga you see. I heard the rumors and the story about you and Carl, so tell me one reason why I shouldn't walk out of here right now."

Shay said, "I was with him only because I needed to survive until you come home, and he told me that he was gone tell you about it when you were at the county jail, but he never got around to it, Tee."

"Well, I feel like you are full of shit, and that is my final word outside of this, so bye, bitch."

Then Tee got up and walked out of the visitation room feeling relieved. When Tee made it back to the pod and went inside his cell, he thought about what just did. Then he smiled with the notion of happiness at last, and then one of the other prisoners asked him for a soup.

Tee told him that he ain't got nothing to eat and went into his meditation so he could have that inner peace because of the way this jail treated people. He knew that the jail was devious and cruel, which made Tee change his whole persona since he got to deal with this for the next few years.

CHAPTER 14

It's March 1, 2008 and Tee just got out of prison. He walked out of those gates and it's like everything is weird because of the years he had just done. All of his homeboys has either gotten killed or busted for drugs, especially the one homeboy that he respected the fullest, which was Jay, his ace boon coon.

Meanwhile, Tee knew that he could not mess up or he would end up in jail again, so he begin his day by attempting to go back to school. He look in the Yellow Pages and seen Remington College and called them immediately.

As the recruiter, Leah Scott, answered the phone, Tee asked, "What I have to do to enroll in class?"

Leah stated that he could come visit the school on Friday, March 15, 2008 at 2710 Nonconnah Boulevard so that they could file the papers to get him enrolled in business administration for the spring classes on April 21, 2008.

Since Tee finally got in school, he met this beautiful chick who was banging from head to toe. She had the type of ass that was so round you could literally sit a bottle on top of it. Tee wondered if he should make his way over to her, and then he wondered if he should ask her if they can become acquainted. But he thought about how much she remind him of Shay, so he went on his way.

Once he arrived in his classroom, he spotted a childhood friend he knew from grade school. His name was Liston Thomas, but Tee called him L.T. for short. They begin to catch up with old memories of how they were tossing girls in high school as well as in the gym locker rooms.

"It's really cool to reunite with my homeboy, and now we can truly build an entourage like we had in high school," L.T. said. How about this, Tee?"

Tee replied, "What's that, L.T.? Don't you see that girl over there with the bodacious ass?"

"Yeah," L.T. stated.

Then Tee replied, "What about her, homie?"

"She look like your high school love Felicia Hughes aka Cappuccino."

Tee and L.T. left school and they went their separate ways, so Tee phone rang while he was headed to his Mercedes Benz. He seen P-Bands!.

"What's up, cuz?" Tee stated.

P-Bands replied, "I need you to come to work with me this weekend if you are down for making a little change, and I know that you're in college now."

Tee said, "How do you know that, cuz?"

P-Bands said, "My wife go to Remington with you and she said that she seen you with this other dude talking about her."

"You mean to tell me that she saw me looking at her? Cuz, your wife is totally banging, and I am very apologetic for looking at her in that way, homie."

"It's okay. I get that all the time," P-Bands stated happily.

Tee then replied that he will work with him this weekend and drove off.

Right after he pulled off from the college Tee's phone rang loudly, and this time it was Shay. He said to her, "What the fuck you want, and why are you calling me, traitor?"

Shay replied, "Baby, I had to do what I could to survive, and that's why I hooked up with Carl while you did your time. Will you forgive me for not being there for you like I was supposed to? Baby, I'll do anything you want me to do, I promise, Tee."

Tee told her that he's done with her and that time is money and money is time, and he hung up in her face without any sympathy at all.

Tee jumped into his CLK 300 Mercedes Benz and drove off as he headed to the crib to pick up some weight and the strap that Jay gave him for a mission before he went to prison. Tee took it with him to go make a serve to a nigga Jay plugged him in with while he was in prison, and his name was Mike. He's from East Memphis, but originally from the Bay area in Memphis 10.

This was his ace in the hole because of the business mind he possessed as Tee's li'l homie. It truly showed Tee that Jay was real and that he cared for his big homie to the fullest.

It's 4 p.m. in the evening when Mike and Tee pulled up at the Trap house in Lake Pointe off Winchester and Tullahoma, which is where they normally meet up at to do business.

While they conducted their business Tee said, "There are so many freaks in there getting high and having sex high as hell. I'm about to hit the highway with these whores and get paid."

"Homie, I'm pimping now, and you, me, P-Bands, Jay, and L.T. can hit Atlanta and let these bitches go for what they know in the strip clubs or on the streets, cuz."

P-Bands told Tee that his wife runs the shaker in Arkansas and Illinois, so Tee replied, "I have a few connections in Atlanta, Minnesota, and California." Tee then called Jay, L.T. and the other homies and told them about the trip.

Jay told Tee that he's gone get Stephanie, Keisha, and Tonya to come with them because those whores been wanting to pull capers like that for a long time.

Tee said that he'll get Caramel mocha, Diamond, and Cappuccino to come too, as well as rent a van.

So, Tee and his entourage loaded up in the van. Tee seen Shay and Carl walking down Peres Street at Hollywood intersection at the wee of the day. Since her and Tee have been separated for years, she has been with Carl. She became shit to Tee because she broke his heart. So, Shay picked up her phone to call Keisha to see what is up. Keisha couldn't make it to the phone because she had so much dick in her mouth and one in her ass as the phone rang.

Shay hung up and tried to call Tee, but he wouldn't answer it either, so she just gave up and continued to be in guilt and turmoil.

It's 3 a.m. in the morning, and Tee just pulled up at the club to pick up his new misses, Caramel Mocha, and told Jay to go get Peaches, Vanilla, and Strawberry to come with them to Atlanta. That's when Tee asked everybody, "What shall we call ourselves as a team?"

P-Bands said, "Purple Team Family," and everybody agreed to it and stamped it as their group.

This what Tee had been working on since 2007, and now it's all in place like he wanted it to be for the year of his release from prison. Now that they're on the way to the top again, Tee has one rule as the leader of this family. That rule was that as a member of Purple Team Family you must stay loyal to your Family members no matter what because we are one and one for all.

Tee said, "This is the most important rule of any other that I may have, but this is the main rule that must be followed heartedly and if anyone breaks it, it will be a strict violation for it. So, is we on the same page as Purple Team Family?"

Everybody said, "Yeah!"

"Okay then," Tee replied. "Let's get about this money then and show them how we roll."

PTF! PTF! PTF for life!

After all the things in the world and the things that Tee had on his plate from the beginning, Tee's main objective of his future has made him a cold-hearted person for women. Reason being is because he went from a loving child to a hateful thug. Tee got his heart broken so many times that he decided enough is enough and started keeping his feelings out of the question when dealing with women.

In actuality, he became one of the greatest pimps to ever come along. Tee had Cappuccino, Caramel Mocha, Diamond, Vanilla, and Peaches right with Keisha, Tonya, and Stephanie. They always wanted to be with Tee ever since Lanetta had him.

Now that they all can be with him together getting this money and fuckin' him every night really made his life wonderful. Tee was the only one in the Family that they were crazy about. He had it going on to the point that Jay, L.T., Mike, and P-Bands just followed his lead.

Even though he had to serve them 10 years in his past, Tee maintained his plan from the time he was released until he started pimping. He truly had an entourage that was behind him every step of the way. This Family wasn't like the last family he formed in the early 2000s because he made sure that he checked out everyone's history from childhood to an adult.

Tee meant everything he drew up while he was in prison, and he wasn't gone make the same mistake twice. So, he decided to take heed to all the advice that were given while he was in prison.

Tee knew that they will soon come to harass him even though he haven't been in the streets just because of who he was then and who he has become now. The police is still mad about him getting out of them murders because one of the people that got murdered was their family member.

Tee wasn't even aware that he were being set up because when that took place in his past life he just acted on the mission. Now he's on another path of getting his money without robbing and killing, and because of that they want to demolish him this time.

Tee was smarter than he had seem to be in the past, and that is what they hate now. Since Tee gave up his criminal life for a life of pimping, the police want him dead.

CHAPTER 15

Even after serving 10 years in prison and meeting P-Bands, losing his homie Tony for life, and his first love, Tee still was left with one option, and Tee made him a new entourage with P-Bands, Jay, Mike, and L.T.

He finally had the chance to get with Keisha, Stephanie, Tonya, Peaches, Diamond, Vanilla, Cappuccino, and Caramel Mocha. He truly felt good about himself again and he seemed happy now. This was his time to shine like diamonds and allow his wings to spread tremendously since his heart has been mended back together again.

Tee pulled up at his crib realizing how much he went through over these years. As he walked through the door he said to himself, "It's a hard-knock life in those streets." Now it's like get it how you get it and he said, "How people treat you when you down and out is the way you treated others." This is what he has tried to take away from his mind for the longest and continue to move forward as a gangsta.

This was the last time that he was letting a woman get to him or break his heart. He said, "It's truly time for me to be who I supposed to be as a king, and Lord knows that I am."

While Tee decided to take the righteous way of life and then he started meditating on his plans every day.

Shay's life has become a living wreck dealing with Carl and his brother's wife, and Tee still haven't even tried to call her at all.

P-Bands and his wife has given Tee hope and motivation when he got out of prison. They did that by bringing the pimp out in him and when Caramel Mocha came into the picture, Tee felt she was his better half, but wouldn't allow his feelings to get in the way of getting that money from them type of whores. He don't want to experience the hurt and pain he experienced with Lanetta and Shay.

Tee really has enormous feelings for her as well as wanting her to be his wife in the near future, but he know the risk of turning a whore into a housewife. He know that it can't be any different with other professional women in this industry. He thought he have always been taught to love money over bitches.

Tee called and told P-Bands that he really has fallen in love with Caramel Mocha but can't tell her or even give her a signal that he really wants her for himself.

P-Bands told him that he just got to keep his eye on the prize and don't let his head in his pants think for him 'cause things isn't always what they seem to be.

"That's what's up, cuz," Tee replied. "I know that you are looking out for me, Family. By the way, when I get off of work I need you to come with me to handle this little business, cuz."

"Okay, homie. I got your back on this and we can go grab us

some dinner as well 'cause we are going to go to the Soul Shack in South Memphis on Gaston Avenue off Third Street."

"That's cool. Why we're going there to eat, cuz?" Tee asked.

P-Bands said, "That's where my wife's people went since I've known her, cuz."

"Alright, I'm in, cuz, and I hope that they know how to cook some good soul food."

"What you think?" P-Bands replied. "I always go there to eat, homie. Anyway, just meet there when you get out of school, Tee, and I'll show you how I truly get down in these streets now."

Tee hung up the phone and then got back to his school work in business administration.

It finally hit 12:30 in the afternoon and Tee is about to head to the Soul Shack on Gaston Avenue off Third Street. When he pulled up, he seen P-Bands in his 550 SS Coupe Mercedes Benz with Purple Team Family sprayed on the back window. P-Bands had candy blue and gold trimmed paint job with the gold grill in the front and the brains blow and his Benz was the eye of the town.

They walked through the door and sat down and ordered collard greens and cornbread, sweet potatoes, macaroni and cheese, and fried chicken. While they sat there Tee seen this big-ass dude walk in with this ex-girl of his from high school and she said, "Tee, what's up, cuz? Do you remember me, Tee?"

Tee replied, "Hell, yeah, I sure in the hell remember you, Sheena. So, who is that dude you with right now?

"That's my Uncle Donald Smith that use to play football for the Dallas Cowboys when we was in high school."

"Damn, it has really been a long time since I seen him and he probably don't recognize me either, Sheena. I remember that time we went on the craziest spree of shoplifting and stealing cars until we ended up in juvie," Tee replied.

Sheena said, "Yeah, we got our ass whipped really well, but I know that was us being children back then."

"By the way, this is my homeboy P-Bands and this is his wife's family's spot."

"Tee, who is this, homie?"

"This is my childhood girlfriend named Sheena. We did everything together and event to juvie hall together for stealing."

P-Bands gladly told her, "Hello!"

She said with a smile, "Hello to you too. It's nice to meet you and hopefully I'll see you again."

"Please keep my big brother out of these streets, cuz."

Tee and P-Bands walked back to their table and sat down to finish they meal, and Tee told his homie that he shall have been good to her in school, but shit happens all the time to the good ones, huh?

P-Bands told him, "We only get what we breed when it comes to women. You need to make the next woman how you want her to be for you, cuz. That's how I got my wife, and she is cool with our way of living, homie. Don't you know that is what a pimp do in these streets? The woman has to know her place in my kingdom and the man must know his woman at all times because most women these days are self-sufficient and egotistical as well as fucked up."

Tee said to P-Bands, "I realize that every woman isn't the same. I will keep in mind that I can't let my guard down."

He knew that is how he ended up in that situation with Shay. Tee has to be harder than he is accustomed to, but until then he must stay focus on his career in business administration.

Tee have been doing good since he got out of prison a year ago, and he hasn't been into any trouble since then. He still hasn't got Shay out of his system, and it's not gone be just that easy either. Tee knew that he must leave the past in the past as he work on his future each and every day. He loved the fact he wasn't running the streets the way he used to. He felt good about his life at this point, and he hope that his new Family feels good about what he's doing positive at school and at the shop.

Tee is a very smart man when he apply himself to the fullest, and the crazy part of that is he never was an ignorant child, he just experienced the hardest thing as child with his parents' trage-dy. Tee had to fend for himself ever since he was seven years old and all he knew was the streets, and the only reason he knew that were because of his friend's mother, which was Tony. However, Tee always wanted to have a business of his own as well as run a beauty and barber salon with the woman of his dreams, Shayla Smith.

When all that went out the door for awhile he started his life in crime, which hurted him through the years. Tee only experi-enced heartache and pain. Tee had to get it how he lived for the most part and experiencing those paths of life really made him who he are today—a college student that's the leader of a mon-ey-getting team.

Tee truly is loving his lifestyle now that it's easier than before and he can be patient even more because all he do now is pick up money from them whores on his team. He probably bring in about $30,000 to $35,000 a month for all seven of his whores. Tee know that it isn't easy, but somebody got to do it, so they have to do it swift as a gangsta, ya dig?

Tee truly loved the fact that he had whores to get his paper this time, and that is what made him so special and unique to the streets this time around. The only reason is because he did them 10 years in prison he met his new business partner P-Bands. P-Bands showed him how to get paid without the robbing and killing.

CHAPTER 16

Tee said to P-Bands, "Who is following us, cuz?"

P-Bands stated "Punch it, nigga!"

That's when he heard a gunshot racing towards their car. P-Bands ended up getting hit in the back of the arm and leg. He realized that he lost the police and the car that chased them on Elvis Presley Boulevard, so he pulled into the garage and parked. He didn't know who it was, so he jumped into another car.

That's when P-Bands said in a painful voice, "I can't walk, run, or shit, homie, so just take the money with you."

Tee replied, "Are you sure you want me to do that, cuz?"

"Hell yeah."

P-Bands said in another painful voice, "I'll catch up with you later, homie," so Tee ran out of the garage and realized that it was surrounded by cops. He dropped the bag 'cause he knew it was gone slow him down, but as soon as he dropped the bag he felt a sharp pain his neck and back.

Then he said, "I took a bullet in my neck and my back and the pain is still there." When he woke up from the dream he were having, he knew that it was mighty weird and thought he knew it were the devil's trickery. Ever since he changed his lifestyle and his way of living in the streets he's been having those type of dreams.

Tee said, "The dreams always be about robbery and murder." Tee understands that once you change your lifestyle these type of things always comes to haunt you.

Tee really has given up the devilish ways and given up the crazy street mentality for a productive mentality. This came about when he went to that stupid-ass prison in west Tennessee.

At the spur of the moment there were so much that came into Tee's head. He knew the devil were trying to get him to lose out again, so he just stayed focused on the present so that his future could be promising.

Tee depended on Jah this time to prevail over the fiery darts of the Beast that trample under thy feet. Tee was finally living a very hypocritical life outside of promoting prostitution.

Ring! Ring! Ring!

As the phone went for about a minute, Tee picked up the phone and answered it with, "What's up?"

"This is Mike, cuz. I was wondering if you got time to come over to discuss the profits of last month's packages."

Tee replied, "I will have time when I get through doing my project for my business class, and before I come I got to pick up some money from my whores, and then I'll be at the Trap house."

"Okay, Tee," Mike replied, then they both hung up the phone.

Tee started his project first for Mrs. Wright's class on business law. Then Tee presented the law states that every business has to be started with a plan. Tee told the class that they must get trade-marked and patented on all inventions each individual comes up with as their invention.

In his PowerPoint presentation he showed that his profits will go up by the year 2013 and that he would have been in business for 18 months because this were given by using the charts and graphs.

Mrs. Wright said to him, "Very good, sir," and Tee sat down in his seat and waited for his grade. Tee received his grade, and it was a B+. It made him so happy that he was ready to celebrate for the few hours he had left in school for the day. He told his friend in class, L.T., to meet him at lunch to smoke a blunt.

L.T. said, "Where are we gone go to smoke, cuz?"

Tee replied, "To the creek by the hotel. That's where I see everybody go to when I'm coming back from lunch."

"Alright, let's go to the creek, homie."

"Oh shit! Erica wants to come with us and she is fine as hell, homie."

"It's cool, she can come if she wants to L.T. I just hope she down for the thrill that might come up after we smoke. She need to bring that girl she be with everyday anyway because I want to see how her head bobs. She will eventually want to get in the family if we show her the ropes, cuz."

"Tee, you got to be on that right now, cuz?"

"Hell yeah. I am on that all the time, homie, because it's Purple Team Family and we got to get this money by any means necessary."

"I feel you, cuz. I need to get on my pimp shit anyway," L.T. replied. "I been just laying low lately since I haven't seen my girl since she left for a university in Chicago, Illinois, which has made me faithful."

Tee told him, "Just in case you need a little help on your game,

I'll show you how it's done when we go back in the building, homie."

He took L.T. in the cafeteria of the school and the first woman he seen he stopped.

"When can I have your hand in matrimony, sexy?"

She smiled at Tee and then stated with passion, "Right now if you want, handsome."

L.T. were like, "It's that easy, homie?"

Tee replied, "Yes, it's that easy these days."

"Well, it's 12:30 in the afternoon and it's time to leave to go home from school. Hey, what are you about to do now, homie?" L.T. asked.

Tee said, "I got to make a few errands before I hit the crib."

L.T. said he'd meet him at the Trap when he's done and then we will talk about our mission on pimping.

Tee were like, "Alright, homeboy!" and sped off into the sunset. He took his phone and put it on silence so nobody would call him while he is checking his traps. Tee told him that he would get a call from someone and they would interfere with what he's got going at the moment.

When he pulled up at Keisha's spot to college his money, she came out with $2,500 and then she said, "Daddy, I'll have the rest tonight."

Tee replied with, "Why are you short $1,500?"

She said, "You know that he don't come 'til night time every Friday. Why are you here this early anyway, Tee?"

He said, "I just thought I'll make my presence known today since I'm in the neighborhood."

Keisha was like, "That's a first, cuz," and hoped that he did that to everybody on the team.

It's been a long day for Tee and his team, so he took them with him to the Trap house where all of them hang to smoke and get drunk. Jay, Mike, and P-Bands was in the kitchen cooking up that grade a coda, which was that pure cocaine.

While Tee and L.T. was in the living room with all the ladies talking about the capers they're gone pull in Las Vegas, they all knew what Purple Team Family stood for, and that's getting money to survive in these crooked-ass streets of America. But Keisha was kind of like they need to come up with who gone do what before they hit that highway.

Tee said to them, "We have to have one of you all to get a date and make him or her really comfortable because it's gone take finesse to pull this off in Vegas."

Tee had asked his instructor if he came make up for his exams when he get back or can he take them right now? The instructor told him he could take it now if he thought that he's ready.

Tee said, "We can leave after I take this exam," since it were his last one to take before he gets his degree in business administration.

It's 7:40 p.m. in the evening and everybody went to pack up all their belongings while they waited to hit that highway to go to Vegas.

Tee told P-Bands and Mike to make sure that there isn't any type of weapons in view. He told them that going west is the hardest on that highway because there are always roadblocks.

As they were on their way to the west coast towards Sin City to get them some money, they had a few problems with their vehicle, but it was small and could be fixed immediately. The van headlights were dim and needed another bulb for the left side of the van, so Tee pull over to an exit as he got off on Broadway Street in West Memphis, Arkansas.

Tee pulled up at Advance Auto Parts store and purchased a 25-watt light bulb for the brake light on the left side. After he finish getting it installed he pulled off and headed to I-40 West as he looped off I-55 intersection.

When he got towards Texasaw County he stopped to fill up the gas tank since he never filled up in Memphis.

Tonya asked Mike, "Can I talk to you?"

Mike said, "What do you want with me, Tonya? There's nothing a whore can do for me but suck this dick, so is that what you want to do, Tonya?"

"Hold up!"

"Tonya, you want to give me some money or you want me to pimp you out like the Big Homie? Which one you prefer, madam?"

Tonya said, "Mike, you always thinking I'm asking to get with you when all I wanted to say was what do you want to do on this mission?"

Mike said, "Girl, I'm the one with the gun and that is what's going on with the part I play."

"Well, I thought I would ask." She just needed to be safe and secure regardless of who got the gun or who gone pull the date. The only thing is they must have some money, and she's talking about big money.

Tee asked Jay, "Where we want to start at first?" Jay was frequent with the streets of Vegas.

Jay said, "It really don't matter because I've seen all the spots up here and it's time to get richer than hood rich. Drive to the main boulevard and make a right on Alturia Boulevard where the Hilton Hotel is at to let them out right there so that they can seek out their first trick. Once the girls get them where they need to be inside the hotel, then we move in and take the money."

Tee stated, "Jay, is you out of your mind, nigga? We isn't in Tennessee anymore, and if we get caught we are all going to the feds. We need to let the ladies pull them to a remote spot in their car and take everything that way. That's how we can just hit all of them at once, cuz."

"Tee, you are a genius!" Jay was glad to have Tee as the brains of the family.

Tee told the crew that they must do it quick and get back on the highway. Then he said with a smile, "Peaches, make them empty their pockets, and I mean empty them. You understand, bitch?"

Peaches replied, "Yeah, nigga."

Now Caramel and Vanilla asked, "What is our role and where do it take place because our coochies is hot like a firecracker exploding in unison. Ha! But for real, Tee, when do we go?"

Tee replied, "It's you and her turn right now," so they jumped out the van and hopped right into the trick's car one by one.

After pulling this off, Tee and his crew jumped into the van and went to the place they're going to stay at tonight. Tee told them to keep their eyes opened and take a minute to see if they were being followed by anybody since no one got killed afterwards.

Tee told all of them to take their clothes off and change into some different ones and then go burn them in the back of the building where the trash can is. He then said, "The crew need to go get into the van." Once they got into the van Tee cranked it up so that they could get the hell out of Dodge.

Now they're on the highway heading back to Memphis from Vegas and Tee, Jay, Mike, P-Bands, Tonya, Stephanie, Peaches, Diamond, L.T., Vanilla, and Caramel Mocha was laughing and talking about how the robbery went in Vegas. It was cool for a moment, but Tee told them to shut the hell up about that and talk about something else.

On their way to Memphis Tee got off at the exit that said Arizona to fill up the van at the Texaco gas station. While he went in to pay for the gas Peaches had to go use the restroom. While

Peaches went to use it, Caramel Mocha got out with her and they both went to use the restroom.

Tee came walking out the store and said to them, "What the hell you two doing? Get y'all ass back in that van right now."

Peaches replied, "Nigga, I got to use the restroom. Why in the hell you're tripping?"

Tee replied, "We got to get our ass back on this road as quick as possible."

"Alright then, I'll make it quick for you then, Tee."

Then he went to pump the gas. Tee got finished and back into the van waiting on Caramel Mocha and Peaches so they could leave Arizona because they were totally on pins and needles. They had the tricks and the cops looking for them in Vegas, and it was too many people to be running from. They hit a lick for damn near $450,000 in Vegas. The time that they were there wasn't even enough time to have fun because it was in and out.

"What an amazing thing when you have the opportunity to get away," Jay said in happiness. They didn't get caught in Vegas doing the things they did to those tricks.

Stephanie told Mike that she wanted him to be her man for the trip, and Mike said, "Girl, there is no way that I could be your man, but I could be your pimp."

"Ha, ha, ha," Stephanie sighed to him as she told him, "Be for real, nigga. You'll never be able to pimp me or anyone else."

Mike told her wouldn't be a hard thing when she's already a whore. "I could pimp you if I wanted to, but you don't have the skills that I require, and that is charm. You hear me, Stephanie?"

P-Bands stated, "We need to hurry up and get to Memphis so all of them can split this money up. Me and my wife wife can move out of town for a minute until the news stop broadcasting what happened in Vegas."

They all agreed to that gesture and P-Bands rolled up a couple of blunts to smoke. As blunts got passed around the van to each person, Tee stated, "We're right at Texasaw County."

"Okay!" they all stated.

Tee kept driving 70 mph as he finally made it into Little Rock, Arkansas, then he put it to the max. Tee was going 85 mph in a 70 mph zone. He was ready to get in his hometown and back to the Haven.

Now that he made it to the Third Street and Vickers Mississippi exit, he got off and headed to the Gates, which is where one of the traps located in the Haven.

CHAPTER 17

Now that they are back in Memphis, Caramel Mocha told Tee that it's time to mingle like the ocean waves in the ocean.

Tee stated, "I have been waiting on you to say that ever since we were on the road."

She replied, "For real?"

He said in an excited voice, "Hell yeah!"

They went to their house and spent the rest of the night together and then they both jumped into the shower. While in the shower Tee slowly washed her body with a passionate touch. The way that he use his skills in the shower made her want to hurry up so they could get into the bedroom.

During this time Caramel mocha rubbed Tee with the tip of her fingernails, and his body started to shiver from that, which made him get hard instantly. When they both came out the shower they went into their room and he laid her on the bed. Then he took his tongue and licked her neck as he worked his way down to her titties, then he sucked her nipples as she moan in unison.

While he was sucking her nipples, she rubbed his shaft and inserted all of him into her mouth as she bobbled her head up and down. She splurped and spit on him as she sucked the life out of him passionately.

Tee put his dick into her juicy, wet twat and begin to stroke it slow in a circular motion as he felt the warmth of her love over and over again. He heard the moans she were making and reach his peak as he beat that pussy up with no hesitation. This was the best sex he ever felt in his days of misery and pain because when he was with Lanetta, Shay, and Princess, none of them made him explode like she just did.

Tee thought it was like a match made in heaven as he laid there with a wad of money and a bad-ass bitch named Caramel Mocha.

"This couldn't get no better than this," he said. "Why did I ever stop going to the Shaker anyway? That was the dumbest thing I ever could have done."

When he started selling dope and robbing it got him into so much drama with other niggas, so Tee then begin to take his rightful place in the streets as he were taught. Tee was one of the most trusted people in his community, and he did what he had to do to live that life. Even though the ups and downs of his fatal tragedies, he were faced with the beginning of a new chapter and a new lifestyle.

Tee's life really wasn't nothing but hell, but he knew that he did the impossible to build what he had built. He built an entourage that were strictly about that paper.

The phone rang while Tee was laying there thinking of his life and the life he encountered over the years. Since he wanted to change to a better living style he finished college and got his degree in business administration.

Afterwards, he and Caramel Mocha started a life of true love and happiness. Then he ended up getting her pregnant and they had a beautiful little girl. Tee wanted to name her Ashanti Sade Wright, but he agreed to Carmella Sade Wright.

Tee and Caramel Mocha had given up all the streets to be a family of three now. When she saw the ring that Tee had for her it was an immediate "yes!" She said it before he even got his words out to ask for her hand in marriage. They raised their daughter together and ended up getting married around the time P-Bands and China Doll get married.

Now that Tee went straight Rastafarian and became a teacher of black manhood, along with his queen Caramel Mocha he opened up a school of his own. Tee wanted to inspire all the soldiers that were in the streets because he have been in their shoes quite a few times before and this were him giving back to the community.

Since he had the opportunity to change as he were listening to other black men in his hood, he probably wouldn't have lived the way he did in those crooked streets.

Tee's phone rung and he answered it by saying, "Hello, who is this?"

"This L.T., homeboy. What are you doing today? How are you doing?"

Tee replied, "I'm doing good, and it has truly been a blessing to hear from my old friend since we last kicked it."

"Well Tee, I have been busy with the work I'm into right now and I haven't had the time to get free because of that, homie."

"It's cool, homeboy, because I am just raising my little one."

L.T. said, "Little one? You had a baby by who, homie?"

Tee told L.T. him and Caramel Mocha had their first child.

"What, what, what? You mean to tell me that you and she hit it up like that after we finish that work?"

"Yes!" Tee replied. "Cuz, she had the best pussy and she was twerking that pussy on me."

"Man, that some shit. Tell me about it, homie."

Tee said, "That is what I love about her, and she gets money so I won't have to be in the streets anymore."

Tee's friend L.T. told him, "That what's crackin', homie. It's good that she's keeping you out those crooked-ass streets because I'm glad to see my homie on his grown man shit."

"Now it's time that all the other homeboys and homegirls get their stuff together. We have been doing this shit for so long that I am very happy for you, Tee. This is straight from the heart, cuz. I just hope that you raise your daughter right like the queen you need her to be and that you don't let no one use or abuse her, homie. You are a true friend, and you keep everybody on that family shit more than any other friends I've had, cuz."

Tee replied, "L.T., you are truly like a brother that I never had, and to let you know from the heart is totally a plus, homie." Tee got a little sensitive when he said that to L.T., but he meant every bit of it. Tee was a gangsta-and-a-half and he still was, no matter what.

P-Bands called his homie Tee to check on him since he haven't heard or seen him outside of that day they hit that lick in Vegas. When he answered the phone he said, "Hello?"

"What's up, homie?" P-Bands asked.

Tee stated, "Just sitting back with my daughter chilling while baby is working, homie."

"And how has it been between you and her since I fix you all up when you got out, homie?"

"It's been gravy!" Tee replied. Then he stated, "She is a good wife to me, P-Bands."

Then P-Bands replied, "I really can say that he love her more than he ever loved any woman in his life." P-Bands said that he could always imagine that they would be a perfect couple and that what they became together was the perfect couple.

Tee wanted to laugh but he knew it were true, so he just stated, "You damn right, cuz. That perfect couple forever and ever more."

P-Bands and Tee got off the phone and as soon as Tee hung up his phone rang again. "Who is it?"

"This Keisha and I just heard the news from the family, congratulations! You had a baby girl! What is her name, Tee?"

"Her name is Carmella Sade Wright."

"That's cute! So, when are you gone have your black awareness seminar?"

Tee told her it will be this week at 10:30 a.m. and it's gone be at the park on Winchester off Boeingshire. He said that he will be teaching on the natural living of Afrikaans as a whole on H.I.M. Haile Selassie I, the 225th descendant of King David and the Queen of Sheba dynasty.

Keisha said, "That's what's up. I'll be there with flying colors of that red, black, green, and gold attire."

Tee replied to her, "I'm glad that you stop being the freak of the community. A queen keeps herself fit at all times, as well as stays conscious about who she is. You must know where you came from also."

After that she told Tee thanks and hung up the phone.

Tee heard the car pulled in the garage and ran to see his wife, and as soon as she got out the car he kissed her and their daughter kiss her as well. Tee was so crazy about his wife and best friend that he was truly faithful to her 110%.

Tee had her dinner and her bath water ready as she went into the house like a real king is supposed to do for their queen. A lot of niggas would say that it's weak, but Tee know the essence of a king and how to be so true to his words. Tee is the only man to ever treat Caramel mocha the way she have gotten treated. He is so loving to her, and she is so loving to him, as well. They are the perfect couple.

However, Carmella starts to cry for her bottle and Tee rush to the refrigerator to get it as quick as possible. While Caramel was in the shower and washing her body Tee went on to burp his little princess. It's been a long time since he had to burp a child, and to have his own child made him feel so good to be a parent.

Caramel Mocha got out the tub and stormed to the kitchen to eat that fabulous meal that her king cooked. She told Tee that he's the best cook in the world and that he need to open up a restaurant and to call it The Blue Diamond Bar and Grill.

Tee said with a smile, "You sure is right, my love." Then as they sat at the table eating that delicious meal he told his wife that he got to go to his seminar in about an hour or so.

She said, "Baby, you have made a tremendous turn around, and I love you for that, my king."

Then Tee said to her, "Baby, it's all because of you and our little princess that I stay out of the streets. Now that I'm finished with college and have my family that's all I need to get where I want to be in this life of struggle."

Tee graduated with honors in his class and all the people he knew around Memphis was so happy to see him make a complete turn of his life of crime. They knew how he were at one point in life and that's what cause him to be more attentive to his future.

CHAPTER 18

Jay was out on his porch and seen that the cops were circling around his street. He seen that Peaches and Keisha was out there on the block selling that wa-wa when the cops stopped and got out their car.

When the police seen Peaches on her knees and Keisha bent over the trash can while Carl and Tim was busting and getting orally sexed, the cops stop them in the act.

Jay was like, "Damn! Why are those dumbass whores doing that shit right in front of the breezeway? They know better than that shit. Now I'm gone have to go get their ass out before Tee finds out that their ass is going to jail for prostitution."

So, Jay headed to the bonding company and he told Kathy to make their bonds as quick as possible. Jay knew that they got a seminar to make at the park off Boeingshire in the Haven.

Kathy made their bonds and rushed the paperwork over to the jail, and around about 5:30 p.m. they came walking out of Jail East as they seen Jay sitting there waiting for them.

Jay replied, "Let's go, y'all. We have to make it to Tee's seminar as quickly as possible. We have to get things in order for the whole graduation. Tee is about teaching the youth and young adults how to respect themselves and how to honor thy brethren. We have to hurry up, girls, and I mean hurry up, y'all."

"What are the things he use to get people motivated?" Keisha asked. "That Tee talk with authority and firm knowledge about self and consciousness. He told me that I needed to stop selling my body and adapt to my queendomship as the woman of the universe. Tee is truly the essence of a changed man in our community."

When they all got there and sat with each other they listened to every word that Tee spoke because they knew where he had come from and where he were trying to go as a king in his kingdom. Even though Tee was still over them as their leader and they all respected him with great respect, they knew that he would give his life for them if he had to, and they would do the same for him.

Keisha said to all the Purple Team, "We need to go up there and speak on the things we did in our life so that the youngsters can know that life isn't a game or to be played with either."

They all said in unison, "Hell yeah!"

So, they went to the platform and asked Tee for the mic, so Tee gave it to Jay. Jay spoke about how he was force to live a life of crime in the midst of deception.

Keisha spoke on how she had to sell her body to survive because she had mouths to feed. Her job wasn't enough to get by on.

Peaches said that she and her sister Pebbles had to shake their ass to survive in the wee of the day because they had no funds to pay their rent or buy them food either.

Mike and his brother told them that their mom was on crack and that they joined a gang called Grape Street in order to make it out there in them crooked streets. Mike and Tee were brothers and they never knew it because their mother was out there in the streets for a long time until someone killed her. That's when they realize their stories matched as time progressed.

Tee was so happy to hear that Mike was his estranged brother and told him that they have a lot of catching up to do when the time permits.

The time was flying, so Tee wrapped it up and told the audience to get them some refreshments at the hotdog stand and that the stand was in front of the lot over by the pine tree.

As everyone were leaving the park, Tee, Mike, Jay, Peaches, Keisha, and all the other youths and young adults got into a brawl over something small.

Tee then said, "What the hell is wrong with this fuckin' generation?" He wanted them to be on unity and honor amongst their fellow man but instead they want to kill each other over nothing. Tee couldn't believe his eyes when he seen that they wasn't gone stop the racket, so he just told his crew to come on and head out to his crib to see their goddaughter.

When they made it to the crib they got out their cars and Tee's wife and queen came out with their little princess Carmella Sade Wright. Carmael Mocha said, "How are you all doing today?"

They said, "We're all doing great after hearing Tee speak on consciousness and respect along with honor for your fellow man."

"Okay! Well, I guess you all can come on in to this big dinner I cooked for Tee," and they all went in the house.

Jay told Caramel Mocha that he haven't had a meal that was

cooked in a long time, and she thanked him.

"We must continue to stay like a tight family shall be in this crooked-ass world we are living in, cuz." The reason Jay said that is because there's nothing as loving as a true family.

"To PTF for life!" they all said at the table, smacking their jaws on steaks and potatoes. Then Stephanie knock on the door and they told her to come in.

Caramel Mocha and Stephanie became the best of friends during the time that Tee formed Purple Team Family. Stephanie asked, "What are you all having here, cuz?"

Tee replied, "We are having a little family meal that my queen cooked for her king, and it's finger-licking good."

"Baby, let Stephanie in so she can get her a plate and sit down with the family." So, Tee got up to let her sit down at the table with them.

Right when he did that he heard a horn outside blowing and went to look to see who it was. It was China Doll and P-Bands pulling up to see Tee and Caramel Mocha. When they got out the car and seen that everyone was over there they said, "Wow! We didn't expect to see all of you all over here today."

"What in the world has been going on lately, Caramel?" China Doll asked.

She said, "Nothing much, girl. Just raising this little girl of mines. Also, I want to thank you for hooking us up when he got out of prison too, girl."

"You are welcome, child."

Tee told China Doll thanks as well because he knew if it wasn't for her and P-Bands then they wouldn't even be together at all.

Now that they were through talking, P-Bands and China Doll got them a plate and sat at the table with everybody. Tee then stated to everybody he's glad to have made it through with the ones he loved, grind, and given his life and time to them faithfully, especially when they started to walk in the shoes of a gangsta. "This is what Purple Team Family is about, and this is what we will stay about," Tee replied to the fam.

Tee then told them that it's a new revolution to handle in this crooked-ass world we live in and that they must continue the legacy of their ancestors 103 percent and not play with the path of love and happiness.

Caramel Mocha said to her husband, "Life only changes when there is someone that humanitarily work towards the mark of change."

Tee agreed with her and said to all the team, "It's true."

CHAPTER 19

Now that Tee had heard that the government is after his team, him and his wife Caramel Mocha wasn't about to fold in the midst of the pressure.

Tee asked his wife, "What shall I do about telling the family?"

She replied, "Just go ahead let them know the business, my king."

See Tee called P-Bands, and when P-Bands answered the phone Tee told him to get the team and come to his house right now.

P-Bands said, "Okay," and then hung up the phone.

P-Bands told China Doll to come on because he got to go get the whole team as quickly as possible. As they loaded up in the truck P-Bands pulled off and headed to Jay's spot in South Memphis. Once he got off the Lamar exit and turned on Airways, he pulled up to Jay's house banging that Pac "Ghetto Gossip," and then P-Bands blew the horn.

Jay then ran out the house and jumped into the whip. Jay said to them, "What's up, cuz?"

P-Bands and China Doll replied, "Tee said that he need the family at his house immediately."

Jay replied, "What the hell is going on this quick that he need all of us right now?"

"We don't even know either, cuz, but that's probably why he want us to meet him at his house ASAP."

"Alright then, homies," Jay said happily as he listened to Pac playing in the CD player system that banged with mega bass.

P-Bands pulled off as they went on to their destination and were still wondering what happen so fast that they got to have this meeting.

Well, as they got on to the expressway he headed to Tee's house in the Haven, so China Doll told her man to stop at the store on Winchester so she could get some beer to drink. When they made it to Tee's house, P-Bands, Jay, and China Doll walked in Tee's house to find out what's the problem.

"Hey, everyone!" they said as they seen the whole team. Then they spoke to Tee and her best friend as they sat at the table.

Tee said, "The government is trying to take us down because they saying we are getting too unified. The government just mad because we isn't around here killing and selling drugs anymore. They can't make any money or have a job because the crime is low and the main blocks are clear because our people are now race conscious and they hate it, family."

China Doll said, "That is what the government do when they see unity. They want us to stay divided amongst the masses, but you have to continue your mission, Tee."

Tee replied, "You are right, China Doll. That's what this meeting is all about, cuz.”

Caramel Mocha said, “We must stand for the rights of our family and our people without any ceasing.”

Tee told them, “All of you are right about the way we got to be towards these critics and hold our own 103 percent and never less, homies.”

They all agreed to his lecture as he begin to speak on the time when Benito Mussolini invaded Ethiopia in 1935, but H.I.M. Haile Selassie I conquered Italy’s plan with the genius of the maroons and the buffalo soldiers. “This is how our ancestors overcame the defeat of the invaders of their country just to stay independent and free from the Roman rule under the Pope John Paul I.” Tee was very knowledgeable and had the mind to achieve whatever he liked.

The day of the feast was at hand in 1966 when Dr. Karenga started Kwanzaa as an Afrikaans holiday in America. This was around the time that Dr. Martin Luther King Jr. marched for the human rights for our people to be equal as the rest.

Tee knew history was some of the race’s weakness, but he said that he was gone open their eyes to the truth no matter what happens. Tee told the fam that, “All our people needs to know about the things our ancestors went through in those days. On the day of November 19, 1865 General Sherman Granger went to Galveston, Texas to furnish information to the slave masters that slavery was abolished. However, the truth of the matter was that the 13th Amendment wasn’t never declared in policy until 100 years later from the time they claimed Abraham Lincoln ratified the 13th Amendment.”

Once he told his family that enlightenment, they said that is why they must stay on the path of their ancestors and keep the next generation on the same path that’s coming behind us in this millennium.

Keisha stated with the voice of a bird singing that, "The government is using welfare and food stamps to keep us from the main purpose of political realms."

Right after Keisha said that Tee acknowledged her for her attentiveness and her listening to everything that he taught her in those seminars he had at those parks.

As they were talking about all of the things that took place back in the 1930s 'til the late '70s, which was then politics became war without bloodshed instead of war with bloodshed.

Now that all of the family is ready to establish their path as they push unity amongst all people and take it into account that the government will try to seize all of their assets, they filed for independence as a sovereign nationhood.

Tee told everyone to be careful and stay on the lookout for anything that's unusual and that's not normal. They all agreed and walked to their cars and trucks.

As the team left his house to get back in their daily routine, Caramel Mocha and Tee had a trip they were going on with their daughter Carmella. She had just turned three years old, and she was something to deal with, despite her parents.

Carmella asked her parents if she could have a pair of shoes when they get to the shopping mall in Cordova. A three-year-old that's conscious and aware of the world's bullshit! She was really adorable and amazing to see with her little cute self, but all in all, Tee didn't play with anyone about his child or his queen, so to step up on their porch would be foolish.

This is how Tee was from the time he were born in October of 1978 and his mother and father were experiencing the same things he is attempting to put a stop to as we speak. The only difference is that back then everyone were together regardless of where they were from. Now Tee and his crew was on that mission to get that done for the millennium, but it's not gone be as easy as people think it is with young people.

Tee told his wife that he gone make amends with his ex-girl-friend Shay and her new beau Carl and try to reconcile their differences. Caramel Mocha said, "Baby, you shall have been trying to do that with them because I really think that she and he would be beneficial to this family as well."

Tee was so in love with Shay that he had to thank you for her part in helping him change his life. Tee knew that if none of the things had happened to him he would have been with Shay and they would have had a child together.

Tee was still being hunted because of the time Lanetta and Corey got caught making love in his house in his bedroom and he killed them for disrespecting his manhood. He thought to himself she had nerve to bring another man into his house and fuck him while he was gone.

Tee prayed that he wouldn't have to deal with that again, so that is why he decided to change his lifestyle. Now Tee is a mentor to the youth and young adults and people still try to bring up his past, but they really can't trip about it either.

Tee and his entourage were unconscious as all the other thugs in their community in those days, but it is why his past is so unique and has experience to motivate others not to walk in his shoes.

Caramel Mocha told her husband that they need to go to holler at Shay and Carl so they could make amends because it's the right thing to do.

Tee replied, "Baby, let's get to going, sweetie," and then they went got into their car. Caramel Mocha and her husband Tee was on their journey towards unity and the truth, as well as a promising life as one.

Tee told his wife, "We must continue the path that we started together and never let our guards down for no one that gets in the way of truth and right."

Caramel Mocha told her husband that, "No matter what goes on in the process of maintaining the joy of teaching the blind about the government and how the government is using people in the United States of America, I gone be right by your side all the way to death, even if it means losing my life too."

Tee was so happy to have a down-to-earth woman as well as a team to back him up on his everyday living amongst the people as a whole. Tee was all about getting things done for the unfortunate as well as those that needed help in his mentoring about life. This what gave him the sense of love and righteousness as a man who made it through the essences of defeat from the streets of hell.

Tee never imagine that his life would be conceded by treachery and trickery until he experienced the crooked system of the prison life. Tee always felt that he needed to be a force for his people, and that's exactly what he did as he made it possible for all of mankind by opening the minds of lost souls in the streets. He knew that his zeal was not in vain as he went outside to jump into his 1972 Chevelle and put on that Bob Marley's "Buffalo Soldiers." He played it as he started the car up and then a thought came in his mind, saying to himself that, "you'll never be nothing," but he laughed it off and stated, "I am a king of the most high Jah Rastafari!"

Then he said, "Who will not agree with my kingdom is my enemy." That's the last thing Tee said to those past thoughts of negativity. Tee told his queen to get ready to go so that they can be on time for their apology to Shay and Carl.

CHAPTER 20

Tee cranked up his whip and put it in drive as they drove off and begin heading to Shay and Carl's house in South Memphis.

While they was on the expressway Carmella start crying and acting a fool in the back seat. Caramel Mocha told her, "Hush! Hush!" and she stop crying instantly.

Caramel Mocha asked Tee if he think that he could deal with Shay. Tee replied, "Hell yeah!" even though Tee once had feelings for her. "You can be there too if you want to, sweetie, because I don't want you to think that I'm doing something crazy."

She then asked, "Are you sure you want me to follow you, babe?"

"Yeah, babe."

"Okay then, my king."

So, they both went to the house and went in with a smile on their face holding their little princess Carmella.

When they knocked on the door, Carl came to it and said, "Who is this knocking, Shay?"

Shay said, "I don't know who it is, just open it."

When he opened the door he seen Tee with his family and told Shay that it's Tee and his family. Shay ran to the door with a smile and said, "Hello, you all! What brings you here today, Tee, with your family?"

Tee said, "I came to tell you that I'm very apologetic for how I treated you and Carl, and I just wanted to move forward without any more drama."

Shay said, "Tee, I never meant to hurt you or run out on you like I did, but I had to do what I could for me."

Tee replied, "There's no hard feelings, Shay, that's why I'm here to tell you how apologetic I am about that situation and to see if you and he want to roll with me and the Purple Team Family."

Shay said, "We would love to be with you all for a righteous cause with our people, Tee.

"This was the best thing to do," Tee said happily.

When they finished talking to each other, Shay and Carl said that they want to see how much Tee have changed as a person. Tee, Caramel Mocha, Carmella, and Shay along with Carl walked out of Shay's house and Shay and Carl told Tee and his family goodbye.

Once Tee and his family got into the car to leave, Tee told his wife that it was great to see that they didn't hold any grudges against him. "This have truly become a wonderful time in my life to truly build an empire to fool the government on this mission to have a black nation for our people called the Purple Team Family, which is for the purpose of Jah Rastafari."

"Rastafarian is the rock that created the path for our ancestors and ancestry because of the king of the Jews, the black Jews of Medieval times called Falashas, which was considered groundbreaking for people of Afrikaans in the Eastern world who was the black Israelites in the Holy Bible."

Tee knew that all of his people shall know that the government is still using these myths to blind our people with this spookism called Submissive Attire, meaning to refrain from seeking who you are and where you came from as a black man.

During this seminar Tee taught the people of the world about the essence of the government. He also taught them to have unity in their hearts instead of violence. They felt like the government is the only way to overcome this obstacle, but to be honest with them it is self-perseverance that helps you to overcome adversity.

After Tee spoke these prophecies with great virtue and authority, he and his wife started to leave out the park with their little princess Carmella. Tee and his wife knew that the government was after them, so they had stayed in touch with every one of the family and all of them said that they were fine.

When they left the park, Tee thought over his life again so he could write about his experiences and his story on what brought him to be a man and not a boy anymore. What you can see is that Tee was a knowledgeable and unique person that went through the fire and the storms of life with a purpose from the streets to the sanctuary. Tee's journey wasn't an easy one at all, but his willpower to achieve greatness never ceased to amaze anybody. He were the light, and when he didn't know that he were the light of the community he endured to the end and set the path for the next generation. As his seed grew up to be able to speak clearly, she spoke on the level of her father and her mother.

Tee's daughter were the image of him and her mom, and she kept their legacy going as they got even older. Tee's daughter wasn't the only one who kept Tee's legacy going—Keisha, Jay, Mike, P-Bands, Vanilla, Diamond, and Peaches also did. They was the first family members of Purple Team Family, and they are still pushing for the essence of freedom for all generations and our people as a whole.

The government is still using trickery and misery to break the community up so that they can take back all their profits. The only thing standing in their way is Tee and his family tree, the Purple Team Family.

Tee and Caramel Mocha had gotten a house in Atlanta, and when they moved to Atlanta to further their ministry, Tee ran into some problems with the government because he was doing the work of Jah Rastafari. Tee had never stopped the mentoring to his people or the youth and young adults in this world, that's why the government wanted him so bad.

Tee was like the Malcolm X of today's times because of the teachings of Marcus Mosiah Garvey and H.I.M. Haile Selassie I. The government hated him because of his leadership and poise to achieve the impossible, but even when they burned his house down and sent someone to rape his daughter at age 16, he still pressed forward with his mission.

Tee is doing Jah's work and his queen was right there beside him the whole way to the finish line. Tee knew the outcome of what he had to achieve for the next generation and the generation after that if he were still alive.

Tee said in his own words, "No matter how they treat you when you work hard to rise above the defeat that enslaved our people for so long, stay true to who you are and to where you came from, and then you will know that you are a king by Jah Rastafari. The king is only a king when he has faith in the heavens, which is the heavenly mind that is the truth of everything my brethren and sistren. May the love of Jah Rastafari be upon

I-n-I."

The Purple Team Family became great in the process of diversity and adversity, and the government felt like a fool on their path to gain profits from people who were considered three-fifths of a human being back in the Middle Ages of civilization. This was the time that everybody was saying that Tee and his family will attain the crown of the hood as the image of Jah in the flesh. The reason Tee received that award from his people is that he earned it for his humanitarian work.

Tee and his wife had left that part of their life to their daughter Carmella. Tee's life really became virtue and morally fit with the struggle through these times of adversity when he helped them to see themselves for the truth and reversed the enslavement of the Babylon systems they call an Incarceration Nation.

This story was truly based on the facts and the struggles of Tee's life on the outside, as well as on the inside of the judicial system, as well as the system in these streets. Tee came from nothing to someone that's considered a beacon of light. He also became a force to all by changing his whole style of life for the life of truth, which is why Tee left the streets for the sanctuary.

In fact, Tee had a chance to help everyone in his circle before he ended up losing out on the most important woman in his life, his daughter princess Carmella Sade Wright. Tee's wife Caramel Mocha, who became his queen and a ride-or-die chick, Tee was still preaching and teaching to those who were blind to the government's trickery and fuckery as well as their schemes. Tee was wanted for being too big for the masses of the government with his antigovernment group called the Purple Team Family and the government hated Tee very much.

Tee didn't care because he said, "I will die for what I believe in totally." But as he continue to state this instances of the trinity, Tee seen the FBI watching him and his every move, so he became very cautious.

Ring! Ring! As his phone rang.

He answered it saying, "Hello, who is this calling?"

A woman's voice replied, "This Tonya! Tee, are you coming to speak on the true essence of black consciousness with all the youth in my neighborhood?" Tonya asked happily.

Tee replied, "Yes, I will, Tonya, my sista!"

After that he called Jay on the phone and told him to get everything to set up at the park downtown near the riverfront.

Tee was a bright person and was totally hard enough to stand against the haters, regardless of what was going on with all the people in the community. Tee killed their inner spirit with knowledge and power, meaning word, sound, and power. Tee became a force to the government, and since he didn't care about what happens, he meant everything he said about truth and right followed by love and light.

Tee wanted a better world after the world that he lived in completely, and he knew that in the '90s that all he had to do was hustle to survive the wickedness of the government, which they all knew. Tee had to let them know about how they came up banging hard to survive the way of living in poverty.

Tee was at the point of returning the favor to Jah Rastafari himself, and that's why death wasn't a problem to him if it come while he were teaching his black people the truth about the government and their schemes.

Tee always had a sense of direction in his life, and as the gentleman of his household, Tee made sure that he and his family was in the position to rise up beyond the trickery of the government. That's why he formed Purple Team Family and taught them to be aware of all the news of their community. This was the purpose of Tee's mission as time permitted itself towards maintaining a successful entity for the people of the United States of America.

Tee had the opportunity to do what he wanted to do numerous times knowing that he was the light of his community. He was a well-known soldier who gain his respect when he stood up for his own on the street life and the government in his life as that king black man that gave his people straight up hope and inspiration. Tee's love will continue to be an essence of light to all people, but to his people forever and ever. This is why he went from the streets to the sanctuary.

The intermediate purpose that Tee had as a man living in the society of adversity made him who he had become in the end. However, after he experienced prison time for robbery, murder, and political warfare, Tee was surely the man to look up to. He was that person that seen the light in the process of destruction. He was not letting anything deter him from his main goal of unity and love amongst mankind. This who Tee were to all his friends that encountered him in this book called "From the Streets to the Sanctuary."

ABOUT THE AUTHOR

My name is Eric "Corleone" Bledsoe, I'm 43 years old, single, and currently doing time for three bogus charges. I was placed in jail on May 21, 2009 and charged with Criminal Assault/Carjacking; then five days later, my charges changed to Aggravated Rape, Aggravated Burglary, and Theft of Property to wit Auto Theft. I have been in prison 14 years and still trying to give my time back.

However, I'm serving my sentence at Trousdale Turner Correctional Center in Hartsville, TN. I was tried by 12 biased jurors and a lawyer that allowed me to get railroaded by the judge and prosecutor who were biased anyway. I ended up being wrongfully convicted for those charges listed above and received a sentence of 53@100% and 12 @ 60% ran consecutively.

Therefore, I'm seeking legal assistance to prove my case was bogus and to show that I'm totally innocent on these charges. Please feel free to contact me at this address for now.

Mr. Eric L. Bledsoe #281676
Trousdale Turner Correctional Facility
140 Macon Way, CB-103
Hartsville, TN 37074

Thanks to all that's willing to help me prove my innocence and please help me attain donations for legal fees. From the author with love, peace and prosperity. May God's blessings unfold in our lives forever. "Thanks again".